Hunt slipped a hand beneath her neck.

She was his Lainie...but different. A woman now, not the girl she'd been. And she was hurt.

"Lainie, darlin', it's me, Hunt. Can you hear me?"

She groaned, then sighed as she rolled over and slowly opened her eyes and stared straight at him.

"You're here again, Hunt," she mumbled. "Are we dead?"

The skin crawled on the back of his neck. Had she been seeing him in her hallucinations?

"No, baby, we're not dead, and I've been looking for you."

She grabbed his hand. "You're really here? My Hunt? You found me?"

"Yes, darlin', I found you. Easy now... I need to see what all has happened to you," he said and pulled a bottle of water and the first aid kit out of his pack.

But Lainie wouldn't let him go.

She couldn't believe he was real.

SAVE ME

NEW YORK TIMES BESTSELLING AUTHOR
SHARON SALA

INTRIGUE

Heroes are everywhere.

Love never dies.

I dedicate this book to the brave ones, who keep putting one step in front of another, even though their lives have been shattered, and their hearts have been broken by the actions of others.

Life isn't fair.

But it's ours to live for as long as we exist.

Harlequin® INTRIGUE™

ISBN-13: 978-1-335-59168-5

Save Me

Copyright © 2024 by Sharon Sala

Recycling programs for this product may not exist in your area.

For questions and comments about the quality of this book, please contact us at CustomerService@Harlequin.com.

TM and ® are trademarks of Harlequin Enterprises ULC.

Harlequin Enterprises ULC
22 Adelaide St. West, 41st Floor
Toronto, Ontario M5H 4E3, Canada
www.Harlequin.com

Printed in Lithuania

MIX
Paper | Supporting responsible forestry
FSC® C021394

New York Times and *USA TODAY* bestselling author **Sharon Sala** has 135+ books in print, published in six different genres—romance, young adult, Western, general fiction, women's fiction and nonfiction. She was first published in 1991, and her industry awards include the Janet Dailey Award, five Career Achievement Awards, five National Readers' Choice Awards, five Colorado Romance Writers' Awards of Excellence, the Heart of Excellence Award, the Booksellers' Best Award, the Nora Roberts Lifetime Achievement Award and the Centennial Award in recognition of her one hundredth published novel. She lives in Oklahoma, the state where she was born. Visit her at sharonsalaauthor.com and Facebook.com/sharonsala.

Books by Sharon Sala

Harlequin Intrigue

Save Me

Visit the Author Profile page at Harlequin.com.

CAST OF CHARACTERS

Hunter Gray—Native of New Orleans, army chopper pilot recently out of the military, never got over the disappearance of the woman he loved.

Lainie Mayes—Native of New Orleans, radiologic technician, lives in Denver. Never got over losing track of Hunter Gray, the man she loved.

Chuck and Brenda Gray—Hunter's parents, responsible for their son's disappearance.

Greg and Tina Mayes—Lainie's parents, responsible for their daughter's disappearance.

Millie—Middle-aged housekeeper for the Mayes family, who becomes Lainie's only ally after tragedy.

Justin Randall—Nurse at the hospital where Lainie works, and the man who tried to assault her and is responsible for her going missing in the Denver mountains during a hike.

Scott Christopher—Ranger for the Denver Park Service, assists in finding Lainie when she gets lost on the mountain.

Charis—Lainie's friend who first sets the police on to the fact that Justin Randall had been stalking Lainie.

Chapter One

July 2011
New Orleans, Louisiana

It was the rain.

It rained a lot in Louisiana at this time of year, but tonight it was nothing short of a deluge—so loud on the roof that it muted the sound of Hunter Gray's boots as he paced in his room.

He would look back to this evening as the night angels cried, but there was no warning of what was already in motion. For him, it was a night like any other night in his eighteen years of living.

His dad worked on the docks, and always came home from work drunk.

His mother was drawing unemployment, and was already into her third beer of the evening.

Hunt was in his room, thinking about his girl, Lainie Mayes. He lived for the times they were together. They'd had a plan during the entire senior year of high school. All they were waiting for was for her to turn eighteen.

Hunt had a full-ride scholarship to play football at Tulane University, and Lainie would be following in her mother's footsteps at the same university, pledging her mother's sorority. As a legacy pledge, she was a shoo-in.

But Hunt and Lainie lived in two different worlds.

Her father didn't come home drunk. He was a very well-to-do stockbroker. Her mother wore high heels to the supermarket, and had a housekeeper named Millie, who kept order in their world.

Hunt and Lainie were at opposite ends of the socio-economic scale, but their real burden was the hate their fathers held for each other.

WHEN CHUCK GRAY and Greg Mayes were thirteen years old, Chuck's mother married Greg's father. The boys' dislike for each other happened at first sight, and being forced to live under the same roof only made it worse. It carried through every aspect of their teenage years, until Chuck's mother died right after he graduated high school.

Chuck wound up on the street, and Greg was on his way to college, with all the trimmings. Chuck was bitter and homeless, which only added to the hate and resentment between them, until years later, when fate dealt them another low blow. Their children fell in love with each other, and the war between them began anew.

THE CRACK OF a dish hitting the wall stopped Hunt in his tracks. He shoved his hands through his hair, and dropped down onto the side of his bed, listening to the beginnings of another fight. Curses were flying. More dishes were breaking.

He waited in silence as sweat ran from his hair, beaded

across his upper lip and ran in rivulets down the jut of his jaw. He often wondered how he'd even been born into this family. He didn't look like them, which had been another bone of contention between his parents, to the point of Chuck claiming in one drunken rage that his wife had been unfaithful.

That's when Brenda pulled out an old family photo of her Cajun grandfather, Antoine Beaujean, and shoved it in her husband's face.

"Look! This is Papa 'toine, and it's like looking at Hunter's face. Our son is just a throwback, and you're a jackass," Brenda said, and helped herself to another beer.

After that, the olive cast of Hunt's skin, his black brows and high cheekbones, the same piercing gaze as the man from the photo, and the distinctive Roman nose, were no longer an issue for Chuck. But Chuck and Brenda were a big issue for Hunt, and 50 percent of the conflict in which he and Lainie were caught.

Tonight, the windows were shut because of the rain, but since their air-conditioning hadn't worked for months, his shirt was sticking to his body. Finally, he got up and went out onto the back porch. Rain was blowing in under the overhang, but he didn't care. His clothes were already wet with sweat, and it felt cool on his skin.

He wanted to call Lainie. He just needed to hear her voice, but it was dinnertime at the Mayes house, and nobody was allowed to take their phones to the table. So, he stood in the rain, while the war inside the house waged on without him.

LAINIE MAYES WAS the epitome of southern charm. Well-groomed, well-dressed, always polite, born blessed with a beautiful oval-shaped face, long auburn hair that lay in waves, eyes as green as her daddy's money and what Hunt referred to as kissable lips. The top of her head fit exactly beneath the curve of his chin. He was the last piece of her puzzle. That one missing bit that made her whole.

Tonight, she was sitting at the dinner table, quietly and politely awaiting the first course, and listening to her parents, Greg and Tina's "oh so proper" conversation, but she could tell they didn't love each other anymore.

She often wondered if they ever had. Mama had just been a sorority girl at Tulane University who scored a rich man's son. A classic match straight out of the Old South.

But Lainie's defiant stance regarding Hunter Gray infuriated them. No matter what, she refused to knuckle under to their demands. She and Hunt saw each other and dated each other, and tried to let their fathers' war roll over their heads. The fact that she and Hunt were now going to be attending the same university made Greg angry, and Tina fret.

On a good day, they offered her bribes to quit him.

On a bad day, they threatened to disinherit her.

But Lainie held a hand they didn't know about, and one they couldn't beat. She was three months pregnant with Hunter Gray's baby, and less than a month away from college.

In two days, she would turn eighteen, the legal age for marriage without parental consent in Louisiana, and they would already be at college before she began to show. It would afford them the distance they needed to escape the lifelong hate of their fathers' feud.

He had his scholarship, and she had the trust fund her grandmother Sarah Mayes left her, which would be hers when she turned eighteen. They'd have each other and the rest of their lives.

When she first suspected she was pregnant, she panicked, and put off telling Hunt, because she was afraid of the consequences it would cause in both families. Then a couple of weeks ago she'd begun spotting, and thought she'd lost the baby. But after the spotting stopped, and she missed her third period, she bought another pregnancy test and used it. The baby was still there! She was happy, but time had crept up on her, and Hunt needed to know.

They'd planned to meet tonight, and then the storm came through. So, then her plan was to call him after dinner, but her phone was upstairs in her room. So here she sat, listening to the rain drowning out the drone of her parents' voices, and speaking only when spoken to, until dinner was over. At that point, she laid down her napkin and looked up from her plate.

"Thank you for dinner. I'm going to my room," she said, and stood up without waiting to be excused, and left the table.

The moment she closed the door behind her, she went to get her phone. She always tucked it beneath the chocolate brown teddy bear Hunt had given her on Valentine's Day, but when she thrust her hand beneath the bear, the phone was gone.

Frowning, she began looking around the room, trying to remember if she'd moved it, when the door to her room flew open. Her mother was standing in the doorway with a look on her face Lainie had never seen before, and she was holding Lainie's phone.

"Are you looking for this?" Tina asked.

Lainie frowned. "Yes. What are you doing with my phone?"

"Making sure you don't inform that bastard of a boyfriend that you're pregnant!" Tina said.

Lainie froze. *How did she...?*

Tina's voice began to rise. "I found the box of a pregnancy test kit. Would you like to prove to me you're not pregnant?"

When Lainie stayed silent, Tina started to wail. "Oh, my God! So, it's true! How far along are you?"

"Three months," Lainie said.

Tina groaned. "How dare you do this to me? To us? You've ruined everything, and we don't have much time to fix it!"

"There is no WE, here, Mother. You're not 'fixing' anything, because nothing is broken, and all you've done is lower yourself to digging through my trash."

"Somebody has to protect you from yourself!" Tina shrieked. "I'm having your father contact an abortion clinic. We're driving there tomorrow. You'll be healed before you have to leave for college."

The words were a roar in Lainie's head, and before she knew it, she was screaming.

"You're out of your mind if you think I'll just meekly go along with this! This baby does not belong to you and Dad. It belongs to Hunt and me. We choose. And I'm not going anywhere with you two. You're so full of yourselves and your hate that you've forgotten what love even feels like."

The truth was painful, and without thinking, Tina drew back her hand and slapped her daughter's face. But the moment blood began seeping from Lainie's bottom lip, she took a step back in dismay.

"Oh, honey, I'm sorry. I didn't mean to—"

Lainie was in shock from the unexpected assault, and reacted in kind by snatching her phone from her mother's hands, then shouting.

"Get out of my room. Get out! Get out!"

Tina was already in tears when Greg walked in.

"You will do as your mother said, and no more arguing," Greg said.

The taste of blood was in Lainie's mouth. The imprint of her mother's hand was still burning on her face when she turned on her father, her voice shaking with rage.

"If either of you lay a hand on me again, or hurt this baby I'm carrying, I'll destroy you. I'll tell the world that you murdered your grandchild. Your reputations won't be worth shit, and I'll be gone."

Greg Mayes grunted like he'd been punched.

Lainie knew he was angry, but when his face twisted into a grotesque mask of pure hate, she turned to run.

He grabbed her by her hair and yanked her around to face him. His breath was hot on her face—his voice little more than a low, angry growl.

"I'd rather you and that abomination in your belly

were both dead than have Chuck Gray's bloodline in my family!"

He was raising his fist when Lainie heard her mother cry out—and then everything went blank.

SEEING HER DAUGHTER unconscious on the floor, and now bleeding from her nose and her mouth, sent Tina into hysterics. She began hammering her fists on her husband's back and head.

"What have you done? What's the matter with you?" Tina screamed.

"I don't want…"

She slapped him. "If you ever lay a hand on our daughter again, I will kill you myself. I don't want her to have this baby, but we're going about this all wrong. She needs time away from Hunter, and time to think about her future. I'm taking her to Mother's old place outside of Baton Rouge. We'll tell friends we're going to Europe. We may be looking at having her take a gap year and give the baby up later for adoption."

"Dammit it, Tina, you know what—"

"Just shut up, get her off the floor, then go get some ice. We're leaving now."

"But the storm—"

"You should have thought of that before you cold-cocked your own child," Tina snapped. "Now go do what I said. I need to pack a few things."

LAINIE AWAKENED IN the back seat of her father's Lexus, with her head in her mother's lap, and something cold on the side of her face. For a moment she couldn't figure out what was happening, and then she remembered.

She sat up with a jerk, shoved the cold pack onto the floor and scooted to the other side of the seat. The silence within the car was as horrifying as the situation she was in. She'd been kidnapped by her own parents.

Tina reached for her. "Lainie, honey, I—"

She yanked away from her mother's grasp. "Don't talk to me. Don't touch me. Either of you. I will never forgive you for this."

Tina started crying. Her father cursed.

She turned her face to the window. There was nothing to see beyond the darkness except the rain hammering on the windows, but she was already thinking about how to escape them.

I will find a way to call Hunt. I will find a way to get away.

THE THUNDERSTORM DIDN'T let up, and even after Hunt finally sent Lainie a text, she didn't respond. He didn't know what that meant. She always answered, so he kept trying. He finally gave up messaging in the wee hours of the morning, and when it was daylight, he got in his old truck and drove straight to her house. Even if he had to fight his way in, he needed to know she was okay.

There were cars in the driveway, but her father's Lexus was missing, which was a relief. At least he wouldn't have to face him, Hunt thought, and got out. He rang the doorbell, then waited, and waited, then rang it again. He was about to walk away when the housekeeper opened the door. She was a tiny little sprite of a woman, with a wreath of curls-gone-astray around her face, and she liked Hunter Gray.

"Morning, Miss Millie," Hunt said. "I know it's early, but I would like to speak to Lainie. Is she awake?"

"There's no one here but me," Millie said. "Apparently, they left last night. I got a call this morning that they won't be back. They're taking Lainie to Europe. Some kind of holiday before she goes away to college, they said."

Hunt's gut knotted. "She never mentioned that to me."

"I didn't know anything about it, either," Millie said.

Hunt shoved his hands in his pockets. "Well, thank you, anyway," he said, and started to walk away when something hit him. "Uh, I know this is a lot to ask, but I was wondering how long they would be gone. Would you know by looking in their closets if they'd packed a lot of clothes?"

Millie sighed. She knew about the war between Chuck Gray and Greg Mayes, and knew Hunt and Lainie were caught in the middle. "I might," she said. "If you don't mind waiting, I'll take a look. It'll take a few minutes."

"I don't mind a bit, and thank you. I really appreciate this," he said.

Millie closed the door while Hunt walked over to a concrete bench beside the front flower beds, and sat down to wait. Within minutes, Millie came out of the house and headed toward him, and he could tell by the look on her face that something was wrong. He stood up.

"What?"

Millie clasped her hands together, then took a quick breath. "Their traveling luggage is still here. I'd guess they took a few things, but not anything worth a trip to Europe, and there's blood on the floor in Lainie's bedroom. Somebody tried to clean it up, but it's a mess."

Hunt groaned. "Oh, Jesus. Was her daddy physically abusing her? She never mentioned it to me."

"I can't say," Millie said. "But for the past two years they have fought something terrible. All three of them. Just don't say I told you. I don't want to lose my job. I know they love her. But—"

There were tears in Hunt's eyes. "I know what loving me cost her," he said. "And I know what losing her would cost me. Thank you for the information. And don't worry about your job. I was never here."

He got in his truck and drove away. He didn't know what had happened, but he had a sick feeling in his gut that the dam had finally broken. Neither of their families had been able to keep him and Lainie from seeing each other, but they hadn't counted on being separated, and he had a feeling that's exactly what happened. He finally parked in a supermarket parking lot and sent her one last text.

Lainie, I know in my heart that something is wrong. But I can't save you because I don't know where you are. I don't know what happened to you, but I know it wasn't your choice to disappear. You are my love—my true north, and you always will be. I gave you my heart a long time ago. Feel free to keep it because it's no use to me without you in it.
Hunt

He had no way of knowing that her phone was lying beneath the bed in her old room where it had fallen when her father hit her. Or that she would never see this message in time to stop him from what came next. If he had, he would have moved heaven and earth to find her.

LAINIE WAS LOCKED in the Queen Anne suite on the second floor of her grandmother's old mansion, with no way out. There was no balcony to that room, no trellis to climb down from the only window.

The old estate was a distance outside of Baton Rouge, and had been closed ever since Sarah Mayes's death a few years back. There was still power on the property, but landlines had long since been removed from this house and she was in a panic, frantic as to what Hunt must be thinking.

She'd overheard her parents concocting the story they planned to spread within their social circle, to make Hunt believe she'd dumped him, and now she feared for what was going to happen to her. She walked to the window with her hands on her belly, talking as she went.

"Don't worry, baby, I won't let anyone hurt you, and I will find a way to let your daddy know about you. You be strong for me, and I'll be strong for you."

One week later

CHUCK GRAY WAS the first to see the photo of Lainie and a handsome stranger in the society section of the local paper. They were standing arm in arm on some beach in the tropics, and he took great delight in throwing it on top of Hunt's bowl of cereal as he was eating breakfast.

"Look at that!" Chuck said. "You've been moping around like a baby, and I told you she wasn't worth the trouble. She's already moved on."

Shock rolled through Hunt in waves, but the longer he stared, the more certain it was part of the lie.

"That's not Lainie," Hunt said.

Chuck frowned. "It, by God, is! Look at her face!"

"Oh, that's her face, all right, but that's not her body, and believe me, I know." Then he shoved the paper off the table and finished his cereal. "I've got to go. I'm going to be late for work."

"Sacking groceries," Chuck said, sneering.

Hunt didn't bother arguing. His dad was mean when he was drunk, but even meaner with a hangover, and he wasn't in the mood to deal with it. He'd already shut down every emotion he'd ever had to keep from losing his mind, and was barely going through the motions.

He was heartsick all day, but he could sack groceries on autopilot. When the day finally ended without a message from Lainie, he clocked out, then bought a rotisserie chicken and potato salad from the deli to take home for their dinner.

On the way home, he detoured by the Mayes estate, but the old mansion looked abandoned. He didn't have to check to see if they'd come back, because he couldn't feel her anymore. She was lost, and he didn't know how to find her. All he could do was hope they'd reconnect next month at the university.

When he pulled into the driveway at his house, his

dad's car was already there. He frowned, then grabbed the sack with their food and went inside.

They were head-to-head at the table, whispering in hasty, urgent tones, but then the moment he walked into the kitchen, they hushed.

"What's wrong?" he asked, as he set the sack on the counter.

Chuck and Brenda had already agreed not to tell Hunt about the shocking phone call from Greg. It was better he didn't know Lainie was pregnant, and that they'd taken her away to get rid of it.

So, Chuck shrugged. "I got fired. Drinking on the job."

"And you're surprised?" Hunt muttered.

Chuck shrugged. "I don't know what changed. It's never mattered before," he muttered. "Anyway, you're gonna have to pick up the slack until I can find work again."

"Like hell," Hunt said. "Every penny I make is for college. You get your ass down to the unemployment office and sign up, and Mom can stay sober long enough to make it through the day shift at any number of restaurants in town. This is your mess, not mine."

Chuck jumped to his feet and started toward Hunt, his fists doubled up and ready to brawl, when it dawned on him that Hunt was a head taller, muscled-up to hell and back, well past the age of backing down.

Brenda rolled her eyes. "Sit your ass down, Chuck. Son, you got mail from the university," she said, and handed him a long, cream-colored envelope.

"I brought dinner. I'm going to wash up," he said, then took the envelope and went to his room. He sat down on the side of the bed, slid his finger beneath the flap and ripped it open, then pulled out the letter and began reading.

Within seconds, he broke out in a cold sweat, then took a breath and kept reading. He read it through twice, then laid it aside and leaned forward, his elbows on his knees, staring blindly at the floor through a wall of tears. There was a pain in his chest, and a knot in his belly.

The university had just rescinded his scholarship, and he knew with every breath he was taking that Greg Mayes was behind it. It was a death blow to his future.

The weight of the world was on his shoulders, and when he stood, it felt like he'd aged a thousand years. His steps were dragging as he washed up and went to the table. His mother had cut up the chicken and put a spoon in the bowl of potato salad. She handed him a plate as he walked by. He put some food on his plate and put ice in a glass, then filled it with sweet tea.

His parents were already moving into their usual round of beer and banter, slinging barbs at each other as they ate, but he was numb. Their arguments didn't matter anymore. Nothing mattered. He tried to eat, but he couldn't swallow past the tears. He'd lost Lainie, and he'd lost his chance to get out of this hellhole life.

He went to bed that night as defeated as he'd ever been. He checked his phone as he did every night, praying there would be a text from her. But there was nothing. He put the phone on a charger and closed his eyes, but all he saw was her face, and the way her breath caught when she came apart in his arms.

HIS PARENTS WERE in their room down the hall, and after all that had happened today, they were as close to sober as they'd ever been.

"You still think it's best not to tell Hunt about Greg's call?" Brenda whispered.

Chuck grunted. "Hell yes. Greg is crazy out of his mind. The girl is pregnant and they're 'dealing with it.' Besides, what good would it do? After all this, they'll never be together again."

HUNT DIDN'T THINK he would sleep, but the next time he opened his eyes it was morning, and it felt like someone had died. He felt sad, and empty, and aimless. He left the house while his parents were still asleep and went to pick up his paycheck from the supermarket, told them he was quitting and then drove without purpose, randomly looking for a miracle. But there were no rainbows left in Hunter Gray's world.

When he stopped to get gas, Jody Turner, one of his friends from school, was on the other side of the pumps. He glanced up when he recognized Hunt's old truck.

"Hey, buddy. Saw a picture of Lainie in the paper. Who's the guy she was with?"

"That wasn't Lainie," Hunt muttered.

"Naw, man, it was her," Jody said.

Hunt looked up. "You think I don't know what she looks like in a bikini? That was not her body."

Jody's eyes widened. "No shit?"

"No shit," Hunt said.

"So, what's going on?" Jody asked.

"Her old man is what's going on," Hunt said, and then looked away, unwilling to talk about it anymore.

Jody finished filling up, then replaced the nozzle in the pump.

"Sorry, man. See you around," he said, and drove off.

Hunt filled up, and moments later got in the truck and began driving around the city, going up one street and down another, saying goodbye to the only place he'd ever known.

He didn't know where he was going, but he wasn't coming back. He drove without purpose for almost an hour before he turned onto City Park Avenue, and as he did, the building up ahead caught his eye. It was a knee-jerk decision that made him turn into the parking lot. He got out of the truck, and walked straight into the office, and up to the front desk.

A uniformed officer looked up, gave Hunt the once-over as he approached and liked what he saw.

"Morning, son. How can I help you?"

"My name is Hunter Gray. I want to enlist."

The officer got up and ushered him into another office.

"Sergeant Morley. We have a new recruit," the officer said.

Morley stood up to shake Hunt's hand. "Have a seat and let's see what we can do about that."

HUNT WENT HOME that afternoon, and walked in on a conversation that ended his last regret about joining the Army. His parents didn't know he'd come into the house and were in the kitchen, each of them with a bottle of beer in their hand, but he heard enough to know the fallout of Lainie's disappearance and the end of his scholarship were connected to what his dad was saying.

"It's all Greg's fault," Chuck whined. "He got me fired because Hunt wouldn't leave his daughter alone!"

Brenda shrugged. "Hunt wasn't chasing her. She loves him, too."

"For all the good it will do either of them now. They're gone and I'm glad. Hunt needs to remember his place," Chuck muttered.

Hunt walked into the kitchen, stared at his parents as if they were strangers, and then walked out again.

Brenda looked guilty, and Chuck cursed.

"Well, now you've done it," she said, and winced when she heard a door slam down the hall.

Hunt was sick all the way to his bones. His knee-jerk decision to join the Army was now his saving grace. The war between the two stepbrothers had destroyed every dream he ever had. He didn't know where he would be deployed, but it didn't matter. He didn't know if he'd have to go to war, or if he'd survive it if he did. But it didn't matter. Nothing mattered without Lainie, and she was lost to him.

ONE WEEK LATER, he was gone. He'd taken all of his personal papers to a lawyer for safekeeping. A birth certificate, a high school diploma, his SAT scores, his high school medals, and the awards that he'd won. And if he survived where he was going, then when he was stateside again, the lawyer would send them to him.

He'd left his truck keys and the letter from the university on his bed for his mother to find. He wasn't telling them where he was going, only where he was not.

IT WAS NEARLY noon before Brenda made her way into her son's room to sweep the floors. The closet door was ajar, and as she went to close it, saw that all of his clothes were gone.

"No, no, no," she moaned, and ran to the dresser. All of the drawers were empty.

There was a knot in her stomach as she turned around, then she saw a note on his bed and ran to get it. But it wasn't a note. It was the rejection letter from the university, and his truck keys were beneath it. A cold chill ran through her, and she began to weep.

WHEN CHUCK WANDERED home that evening from a day of job hunting, she met him at the door, shoved the letter in his face and began to scream. "This is what your war with Greg has caused. He's gone."

Chuck's heart sank when he saw the letter, but wouldn't admit any guilt for his son's absence. "He'll be back," he muttered.

"No, he won't. Because he has nothing to come back for, and it's just as much my fault as it is yours. I condoned your stupid brotherly war. I hope it was worth it because our son became collateral damage."

LAINIE HAD BEEN at her grandmother's house for just over two months, and five months into her pregnancy. Her belly was getting round, and she already felt a tiny kick now and then. She had convinced herself it was a boy, and begged her family to take her to a doctor for pre-natal care, but they'd refused. She was onto their game. They were hoping she would miscarry.

She called her baby Little Bear, because her stomach was always growling, and every day she fell deeper in love with a child she had yet to see.

When she began to show, the only person who saw her body changing was Millie. Lainie refused to talk to her parents, and after a while, they quit trying. They'd brought Millie down to the country house over a month ago, and the moment Millie realized what was happening, she was shocked, but said little about it.

Once Millie arrived, Lainie regained a hope of escape, and began marking her parents' routine. She imagined Hunt was already at the university, so that's where she would go when she got free.

Her father had set up an office downstairs, and worked from home every day. Her mother had given up trying to make peace with her daughter, and wept copious tears daily at the situation.

Millie didn't hide her dismay at what was happening to Lainie, and feared for her health and the baby's health, being locked in that room like a prisoner. After a month had passed, she'd had enough.

It was October 3. A day like all the others as she took Lainie her lunch, but when she saw the dark circles under Lainie's eyes, and her drawn expression, it broke her heart.

She set the tray of food on a table by the window, and when Lainie sat down to eat, Millie put a hand on her shoulder. "What can I do to help?"

Lainie's heart skipped. "Are you serious?"

"Yes. This is wrong. This is criminal, and I won't be a part of it any longer," she said.

Lainie was on her feet, so excited she could barely think. "Can you get the keys to my mother's car? She always keeps them in her purse, wherever that is."

Millie lifted her chin. "Yes, I know where it is. I will do that for you."

Lainie threw her arms around Millie's neck. "Thank you! Thank you! I will never forget this."

"Wait here," Millie said. "I have to get their food on the table. If I come back with the keys, then you'll know they are in the dining room. The rest is up to you. I'm not going to lock your door, but stay here until I get back, understand?"

Lainie nodded, and ran to pack up some clothes. She didn't have money or a phone, but she would go straight to the university and find Hunt. After that, she'd be safe.

Once she'd finished packing, she sat down to wait. It felt like forever, but less than fifteen minutes had passed before she heard footsteps coming up the hall.

The door opened. Millie laid the car keys on the little table by the door and blew Lainie a kiss, then walked away. Lainie shouldered her bag, grabbed the keys, and took the back staircase down to the main level, out a side door, and ran for her life. Once inside her mother's car, she wasted no time, and went flying down the driveway like a bird set free.

GREG HAD JUST taken a bite of shrimp scampi when he happened to glance out to the front gardens, and what he saw stopped his heart. He gasped, choked on his food, and then jumped up and ran.

Tina frowned. "Gregory! What on—" And then she glanced out the window and saw her car speeding away. "What the hell?" And then it hit her! That was Lainie! Tina ran out onto the veranda, screaming at Greg, who was running toward his Lexus. "Stop! Stop! You're going to get someone killed!"

And then Millie walked up behind her.

Tina saw the look on her housekeeper's face, and knew what she'd done.

"How dare you?" Tina screamed.

Millie had her purse over her shoulder, and threw her apron in Tina's face. "No, ma'am. How dare *you*? And I quit." Then she went back into the house and straight out the back to where her little Honda was parked and drove away.

Tina was alone in the house without a way to follow. She was screaming at the world as she began calling Greg.

"What?" he shouted.

"What are you doing?" she screamed.

"I'm going to stop her, that's what I'm doing!" he shouted. "I won't have her shaming our name. Do you hear me! I won't have it!"

The line went dead in Tina's ear! He'd hung up on her!

THE PRIVATE ROAD from the estate to the main road was clear of traffic. Lainie's plan was just to get to the highway and get lost in the traffic. She thought she was free and clear until she glanced into the rearview mirror, and saw her dad's black Lexus less than a quarter of a mile behind her, and closing in fast.

She tightened her grip on the steering wheel, and stomped on the accelerator. After that, everything became a blur.

The hum of the engine turned into a roar. The thick layers of kudzu hanging from the trees and along the fences became a narrow green tunnel, and the road signs were mere blips as she flew past. Twice she skidded into a curve, and then steered out of it, but she couldn't drive fast enough to lose him. And then she glanced into the rearview mirror and the Lexus was behind her! This felt like a nightmare. The mother who used to sleep with her when she was sick had betrayed her. The father who once played dollhouse with her as a child had turned into the maniac in the car behind her. She had one brief glimpse of the enraged expression on his face, and then he rammed the bumper of her car.

After that, everything began happening in slow motion. The car went airborne, like a surfboard riding a wave, and began rolling. At first, the sun was in her eyes, and then she was sideways, and then upside down, and then everything was quiet. She heard the hiss of steam, and someone shouting, and then she was gone.

GREG MAYES RAGE had quickly turned to horror. He was already calling for an ambulance and the police as he braked to a stop. The car was upside down and smoking, and the silence was terrifying. He grabbed a fire extinguisher from the trunk of his car and ran, screaming Lainie's name as he unleashed the contents of the extinguisher. When it was empty, he threw it aside, then knelt and looked inside.

She was hanging upside down, still strapped into the seat, her hair veiling her face. He reached to push it aside, then saw her—and the blood, and in that moment wished to God he'd never looked out the front window. He reached for her wrist, searching for a pulse. It was weak, but it was there.

"Lainie, sweetheart! It's Daddy. I'm so sorry. I never meant for… This shouldn't have…" And then he stopped. She couldn't hear him, and there would never be enough words to take any of this back.

His phone was ringing. It was Tina again.

"Where are you? Where's Lainie?"

"She wrecked the car. I'm waiting for the ambulance." He didn't share the fact that he'd caused it.

Tina moaned. "Is it bad?"

"Yes, but she's still alive."

"Oh, my God! This is all your fault. You and your hate for Chuck," she screamed.

"You're the one who said abortion. You're the one who wanted her 'cleaned out' before she showed up at your precious sorority. You're the one who didn't want to be embarrassed," he shouted.

Tina was sobbing so hard she could barely breathe. "And you're the one who said you'd rather see both of them dead than have her give birth to Hunter Gray's child. Looks like you're about to get your wish!"

"I hear sirens. Shut up and meet me at the hospital. I'll text you which one."

"Well, I can't. There's nothing left here to drive."

"Have Millie bring you," he said.

"She just threw her apron in my face and quit, so don't count on her to keep quiet about this whole mess. We're ruined in New Orleans. We can never go back."

Greg felt sick. The truth of who they were and what they'd done was becoming a painful reality. "I am watching my daughter die, and you're worried about your reputation. Mother of the Year," Greg muttered, and disconnected.

And then Millie's car appeared in the roadway. She braked and jumped out on the run.

"What have you done?" she screamed. "You're a monster! Both of you! Is she alive?"

"Yes, she's alive, and you don't talk to me like that!" Greg shouted.

"I'll talk to you anyway I choose," Millie cried. "I don't work for you anymore, and I'll tell the authorities what you did."

Greg flinched, and without thinking started toward Millie, but she was too fast. She was back in her car and flying past them. He watched in dismay as she drove away. Everything Tina said was already coming to pass.

Millie would talk, but she didn't witness the wreck. Their reputations would be ruined. His lawyer would keep them from any criminal charges, unless Lainie lived to tell another story. But he'd cross that bridge when they came to it.

LAINIE REGAINED CONSCIOUSNESS two days later, to the repetitive sound of soft voices and beeps. She didn't know where she was, or understand what it meant, and slipped back under.

Hours later, she began coming to again, and this time opened her eyes. The light was blinding, and the pain was so intense it hurt to breathe. Her mouth felt funny, and when she licked her lips, they felt swollen. Then she heard someone saying her name.

"Lainie. Lainie, can you hear me?"

She blinked at the stranger who'd just appeared beside her bed.

"Lainie, I'm Dr. Reasor. You're in a hospital. Do you remember what happened?"

She closed her eyes, trying to think past the pain, when she flashed on running from the house.

"Wreck," she whispered, then tears rolled. She felt empty. The baby was gone. She choked on a sob.

"No baby?"

He touched her shoulder. "No baby. I'm so sorry. It was a bad wreck."

"Chasing me," she mumbled.

Reasor frowned. "Who was chasing you?"

"Daddy."

Reasor only knew she'd been in a wreck. Not that she was being chased. "Your parents are here. They've been waiting for days to talk to you."

All of the machines hooked to her body began beeping and dinging, as her fingers curled around his wrist.

"No…never…don't let them…" The darkness pulled her under.

"She passed out," the nurse said. "What do we tell her parents?"

"That she said no."

SCANDAL WAS ALWAYS good press. And finding out that even the rich aren't immune, even better.

When Lainie was finally moved into a private room, her parents were AWOL. She was of age. She didn't need their approval for her own treatments. But they fully understood that since they broke her in every way possible, they were also liable for the costs of what it took to fix her.

Some days she was so miserable she wished she'd died with her baby, and other days she was so angry, all she could think about was getting even. This morning, she was waiting for Dr. Reasor to make his rounds, because she had questions. And when he and his nurse finally arrived, she was ready.

"Good morning, Lainie. Have you been up and walking this morning?" he asked.

"Yes, and I have a question. I need to know if my baby was a girl or a boy."

Reasor put a hand on her shoulder. "It was a boy. I'm so sorry."

All the breath left her body. It took her a few moments to remember to inhale, and when she did, there were tears on her cheeks. "What happened to his remains?"

"They were cremated at your parents' request. I don't know beyond that," he said.

"I have to know which funeral home they were sent to."

He sat down, pulled up her records on his laptop, scanned the text and then looked up. "Schoen and Son Funeral Home picked them up."

"Thank you," she said, and remained silent as he finished his examination, and then left.

Millie had been visiting her every day, and when she came that afternoon, as soon as they'd greeted each other, Lainie blurted out what she'd learned.

"My parents made the decision to have my baby's remains cremated at Schoen Funeral Home. The doctor told me this morning it was a little boy. I always thought it was," she said, and drew a slow, shaky breath. "I need to know if his ashes are still at the funeral home, or if my parents took them. I'm going to call Schoen's and ask if they're there. If they are, would you please pick them up and keep them for me until I get out of here?"

Now Millie was weeping. "Yes, of course. Just let me know if they are, and I'll get them today."

"Thank you. I don't want my parents touching him. I'd ask Hunt to come get them, but he doesn't answer his phone."

Millie felt like she was delivering another death notice, but Lainie had to know. "Oh, honey, Hunt's gone. He's disappeared, and no one knows why. All anyone knows is that he never showed up at Tulane."

Lainie was in shock. All this time she'd pictured him already at school. She didn't understand it. He'd been so thrilled to get that full-ride scholarship to play football at Tulane. Another piece of her life had gone missing.

As soon as Millie left, she called the funeral home, identified herself, and asked to speak to the director, and was put on hold. She was staring out the window when he finally answered.

"Good morning, Miss Mayes. On behalf of everyone

at Schoen and Son, I extend our deepest condolences. How may I be of service?" he asked.

"I was told you picked up my son's remains for cremation. I need to know where his ashes are."

"Yes, of course. Your mother said to keep them on hold and—"

"What are they in?" she asked.

"A small black box. However, if you want to keep, rather than scatter or inter, we have small, ornamental urns for infant cremains."

"Like what?" Lainie asked.

"Ceramic teddy bears in pink or blue. Little brass heart-shaped boxes in pink or blue, or if you'd rather—"

"A blue brass heart," Lainie said. "I'm still in the hospital, so I'll be sending our housekeeper, Millie Swayze, to pick up my baby's ashes."

"Of course. I'll let my people know. All she'll have to do is sign the release form, stating that she's taking them from our premises with your permission."

"And you have it," Lainie said. "Thank you for your help. Millie will be there later today."

She called Millie the moment the call ended, and once the message had been delivered, she put a pillow over her face and screamed into it until she was numb.

A COUPLE OF days later, there was a knock on the door, then as it opened, Brenda Gray slipped inside.

"Lainie, may we speak?"

Seeing Hunt's mother at the door was a shock, but Lainie was hopeful she'd find out where he'd gone. "Yes, please."

Brenda's voice was shaking as she approached the bed. "I'm so sorry for all you've been through."

"Where's Hunt?" Lainie asked.

Brenda's eyes welled. "We don't know. He went into a deep despair when you disappeared, and then a few days after you went missing, he got a letter from the university rescinding his scholarship. A week later, he was gone. No note. No nothing. He left his truck keys on the bed and left the letter for us to see. We don't know where he went, but it wasn't to college. He hasn't responded to any of our calls. We don't know anything. But even after he saw the picture of you and the other boy, he didn't believe it. He said it wasn't you."

Lainie's heart skipped. "What picture? There was no other boy. I was locked in a room in my grandmother's house."

Brenda pulled out the newspaper clipping that she'd kept, as well as Hunt's letter from the university, and handed them to her.

Lainie was shocked by the photo and the letter. She looked up in dismay, her voice trembling.

"Oh, my God! That's not me. That's not my body."

Brenda sighed. "That's what Hunt said. He never thought for a minute that it was. But after the loss of his scholarship, I think he knew your father was behind it, and was never going to stop tearing at the both of you. He had nowhere to go, and nothing to stay for. God knows we didn't give him the family he deserved. We were too busy being mad at each other to see what it was doing to you and Hunt until it was too late. I'm so sorry. Nobody knows I'm here, but I'm giving you the picture and the letter. You deserve to know he didn't walk out on you. He was driven away. We broke him, and I don't think we'll ever see him again."

Lainie burst into tears. She was still sobbing, with the papers clutched against her chest, long after Brenda was gone. Losing Hunt *and* their baby was the final straw.

She had her grandmother's trust fund to help her relocate, and reassess her future. She had to find something that gave her purpose, because right now she was as broken as a soul could be and still be breathing.

ON THE DAY that Lainie was finally released from the hospital, Millie picked her up and took her back to the family home to get her car, and help pack her things. They already knew her parents had stayed in Baton Rouge, so she wasn't worried about running into them again.

"I'll get the suitcases. You go on up to your room," Millie said.

Lainie's footsteps echoed in the grand hallway as she started up the stairs. It was like the house already knew it had no purpose anymore. It felt strange to be back here, and even more so when she entered her room. The bloodstain was still on her floor. She stared at it a moment, then looked away. That had been the beginning of the end. Today was the beginning of her future. Now she had to decide what to take with her.

The first thing she put aside to take was the brown teddy bear Hunt had given her for Valentine's Day. Then she began pulling out clothes and shoes from her closet, and putting them all on the bed, and emptying the dresser drawers.

The picture of her and Hunt was in the wastebasket. Likely, her mother's doing. She pulled it out to take with her. She loved him. She would always love him. Nothing was going to change that. Then she began emptying the drawer in the bedside table, found the charger cord for her phone and tossed it on the bed. She didn't know where her phone was, but guessed her mother had taken it. It didn't matter. She'd get another one, with a new number they'd never know. Then she began taking clothes off hangers and folding them to pack.

Millie returned with four large suitcases and a travel bag. "If you need more, I'll get them."

Lainie sank down onto the side of the bed. "I'm out of breath. I guess I'm not as healed as I thought."

"You're just weak from being in bed so long," Millie said. "You sit, and I'll pack what you want."

Lainie sighed. "I don't know what I would have done these past weeks without you. You have been the best friend I could ask for."

Millie wiped away a few tears. "I have struggled with the guilt of getting you the keys. I never dreamed your father would chase you like that."

"If it hadn't been for you, I would still be locked up in that room," Lainie said. "What happened afterward was entirely my father's fault. I blame them and no one else."

"They got away with it," Millie said.

Anger was thick in Lainie's voice. "I knew they would. I heard about the story he spun. All in my best interests, I believe. And only destroyed two lives and killed a baby to do it."

"The law let them off the hook, but the media and

their friends did not, and that's something," Millie said. "They were crucified in the local papers. I don't think they'll ever move back."

Lainie shrugged. "I don't care. Let's hurry. I want to get out of here as soon as possible."

They were down to packing her shoes when Millie dropped one. As she bent down to pick it up, she saw the corner of Lainie's cell phone beneath the bed, and pulled it out.

"Look what I found," she said.

Lainie turned around. "My phone! It must have fallen there when Daddy knocked me out! I'll try charging it in my car. Maybe there's a message from Hunt. Thank you, Millie! This is the best thing ever! Maybe I'll be able to find out where he went."

Millie smiled. "I hope so, honey. I hope so."

They finished packing, then rolled the suitcases down the hall, with the stuffed bear on top for the ride.

"You better see if your car will start," Millie said. "It's been sitting for months."

"Right," Lainie said, and hurried out to check. She slid behind the wheel of her SUV, and held her breath as she put the key in the ignition. To her relief, it started on the first try. "Thank you, Lord," she muttered, and backed it up and drove to the front of the house.

They put three suitcases in the back, and the fourth one and the travel bag in the back seat. The heart with her baby's ashes was in its own box, and lying on the back floorboard.

"I have to get some stuff out of the safe," Lainie said. "You can leave now if you want. I'll be okay."

Millie shook her head. "I'm not leaving you alone until I know you're ready to drive away. Go do what you have to do. I'll wait out here."

Lainie ran back inside and down to the safe in her father's office. She knew the combination and quickly unlocked it, then sorted through the files until she found the one with her name on it. It had all of the paperwork for the trust fund her grandmother had left to her, her birth certificate, her high school diploma, and her SAT test scores. Then she closed the safe, locked the front door as she left, and dropped the house key through the mail slot.

Millie was waiting by the vehicle with tears in her eyes.

"I'm going to miss you, but I know you're going to bounce. You're a survivor, Lainie. You don't know any other way to be. You have my number. You know my address. I would love it if you stayed in contact, but if you don't, I'll understand. Sometimes a clean break is the only way to begin anew. Either way, I love you, honey, and remember, the best revenge is to succeed when people want you to fail."

Lainie hugged her close. "I love you, Millie, and I'll never forget what you sacrificed for me. Be well, and don't worry about me. I'll be fine."

Then she slid into the seat of her SUV, and put her phone on the charger before driving away. After a quick trip to the bank to empty her personal checking account, and a quick stop at her family lawyer, she left New Orleans. The sun was above her head, and the echoes of dead dreams were behind her.

LAINIE HAD BEEN driving for the better part of five hours before finally stopping in Natchitoches. It wasn't late, but she was too weak to drive farther. She needed food and rest, and found a motel.

Once inside, she dropped her travel bag on the bed and pulled the recharged cell phone out of her purse to see if it still worked, and it did. She ordered food from a local restaurant to be delivered to her room, then sat down on the bed to check for messages.

They were months old, and all from Hunt, with each one sounding more desperate than the last, and all of them taking her back to the night of the storm, relieving her own horror, and seeing his fear for her in the texts. But it was the last message he'd sent that destroyed her.

Lainie, I know in my heart that something is wrong. But I can't save you because I don't know where you are. I don't know what happened to you, but I know it wasn't your choice to disappear. You are my love—my true north, and you always will be. I gave you my heart a long time ago. Feel free to keep it because it's no use to me without you in it.
Hunt

She read it over and over until she was sobbing too hard to see the words, and when she tried to call him, all she heard was a recorded message. *The number you called is either disconnected, or no longer in service.*

After that, the idea of sending a text was no longer an option. She had to face the hard truth that he was truly lost to her.

Wherever she settled, she would get a new phone and new number. It was a scary thought, because then she'd be lost to him as well. But she wasn't losing this text. So, she took a screen shot of it, then sent it to her email and began trying to pull herself back together.

A few minutes later, there was a knock at her door.

Her food had arrived, and tomorrow was another day.

DENVER, COLORADO, became Lainie's final destination. It took her two more days to get there because of her constant need to rest. But she'd spent her downtime on-line, researching nursing schools in the city and looking at apartments to rent.

She had one phone conversation with the family lawyer while she was on the road, and he reassured her that he was well aware of her situation and that everything he did for her was in confidence. He told her to contact him once she was settled and had chosen a new bank, and he would make sure that the first annuities from her trust fund would be deposited in that account, and then twice a year thereafter. The irony of being saved from the grave by the woman in whose house she had been imprisoned was not lost upon her.

Within a week, Lainie had rented a small, furnished apartment and was investigating a nursing school program, preparing to embark on a long journey alone.

The ensuing months were often scary and lonely, and there were days when she was so depressed that she could barely lift her head, but this was her reality, and she would find a way to rise above it.

GREG AND BRENDA MAYES went through their days in silence, or in screaming fights with each other. They didn't know Lainie had been released from the hospital until they received a final bill, and then they panicked.

"This was dated last week! Where is she?" Tina cried.

Greg shrugged. "She probably went home."

"I need to know!" Tina said. "Take me there now!"

"She won't talk to us," Greg said.

"I don't care, dammit! I just need to know!" Tina begged.

They took Greg's Lexus, and rode in silence all the way to their New Orleans home. As they were pulling up, they noticed that Lainie's car was gone.

"Oh, my God," Tina moaned.

"She's probably just out shopping," Greg said, but Tina jumped out of the car and ran, her hands trembling as she unlocked the door.

The first thing she saw when she opened it was a gold key on the floor. She picked it up and turned it over.

"Lainie's house key. It has that little spot of pink fingernail polish on it," she said, and ran up the stairs and down the hall to Lainie's old room.

The door was wide open. Closet doors were ajar. Dresser drawers were half-open, and everything that had belonged to their daughter was gone.

Tina let out a shriek that sent a chill all the way to Greg's soul. The last time he'd heard that sound was the second before their baby crowned during delivery. It appeared the pain of a mother's delivery was equal to the pain of that same child's death. Lainie might be alive in the world somewhere, but she was dead to them, and Tina knew it. He turned his head and walked away.

HUNT'S ARMY APTITUDE tests had labeled him proficient in all the things it took to be a pilot, and the thought of flying Army helicopters was his first choice. Over the ensuing months, he went from Basic Combat Training to Warrant Officer Training School, then to Basic Helicopter training to learn how to fly. At the end of that course, he received his wings and went on to in-depth survival training.

By April of the next year, he was on his way to Fort Bragg for training on the Apache simulators on base. His hand-eye coordination, which had made him a good quarterback, his attention to detail, and a near photographic memory soon put him at the head of the class.

Nearly three years after leaving New Orleans, Warrant Officer Gray was now fit to fly Apache Longbows, the most formidable attack helicopters the US Army owned. But the new had barely worn off his rank when the US Army received new orders.

Troops were being deployed back to Iraq, this time to join in the fight against ISIS. It was a sobering moment of Hunt's existence, and on the day of their company's deployment, he was quiet and withdrawn.

He'd made friends, but none of them knew his story. All they saw was what the Army had made of him, turning body bulk to hard muscle. He rarely smiled, and a quick glare ended the beginning of any argument.

They called him Gator, because of his slow, Louisiana drawl, but it remained to be seen what would happen over there. Would they live to come home? Would they come home scarred and missing limbs? Or would they come home in a coffin?

And that was Hunt's mindset. He guessed he might die there, or come home crippled, but without Lainie, he didn't really care.

Chapter Two

The troops hit the ground running upon arrival. Base camps and communications had already been set up in a vast desert basin surrounded by mountains. The layout was not unlike a wheel, with the helicopters in their own space in the middle, then tent cities and portable buildings laid out accordingly. Medical and medics in their own area. Troops in their areas next to motor pool, and pilots bunking near the choppers that they flew. The entire base camp was fenced, with a single-entry point and rotating guards.

Nearby villages were still inhabited by locals, but after so many homes and buildings had been destroyed by the wars, the survivors lived in little more than hovels cobbled together from whatever was left.

When the pilots weren't in the air, their time on base was about strategy sessions and daily updates from their commanders. Waiting for intel, plans changing on a dime to take down the next group of insurgents.

Troops on the ground dealt with snipers and IEDs, and when soldiers on the ground needed air support, they called in an air strike. For them, the blade slap of

Apache Longbows was better than the jingle of Santa's sleigh bells on Christmas night.

The quick strafe of ammo from the choppers always sent the enemy scurrying for cover. The precision launch of radar-control Hellfire and Stinger missiles blew up enemy tanks and insurgent strongholds.

Hunt's near-perfect record for hitting targets in the simulator had given him the gunner position, which put him in the front seat of an Apache as both gunner and copilot, while the pilot steered from the back seat.

Hunt's pilot was a man they called Preacher. He got the name by quoting Bible verses instead of curses during times of stress.

As the months passed, the violence of where they were had begun to smooth the rough edges of Hunt's grief. Surrounded daily by death, the hunger and hardship of the people of this nation took him out of his own sadness. Humanity was at war with inhumanity, and he was just a heartbeat in the middle of the roar. He still dreamed of Lainie, and made love to her in his sleep. He could still remember the scent of her and the sound of her voice. But he had no tears left to cry.

As the months passed, his dreams became rehashes of battle and bombs, of snipers and death. Of children laughing in a street one moment, and running from gunfire the next. Of witnessing a woman approaching the gate of their base with a child in her arms. They could hear the woman praying aloud to Allah over and over in a high-pitched shriek, while wearing explosives strapped to her body.

The guards had been given orders to fire when she

suddenly stumbled, falling shy of the gate by about a hundred yards. The explosion blew her and her child to kingdom come. It rocked the entire compound. Blew the guards off their feet, and left a hole in the land where she fell.

The sadness and madness of war was never-ending, and whoever was still alive when night came lived to fight another day.

LIKE EVERY SOLDIER, Hunt had long ago accepted that what he did in the air also killed whatever was on the ground. He tried not to think of innocents caught in cross fire, or of the children they sacrificed as human shields.

He dreamed of the hot, humid heat of the Louisiana swamps and woke up to blowing sand and a land so dry the sky looked yellow. It was cold in the winter, with snow and rain in the northern mountains, but cold weather didn't ever stop war.

He missed the drawl of the Deep South, and the Cajun accents from the streets. He missed the taste of Creole gumbo that started from a rich dark roux. It bubbled with tomatoes and okra, had thick, fat shrimps and chunks of andouille sausage, and was seasoned with filé gumbo powder that cooked down to a heavenly stew, then was served over a big bowl of rice. He dreamed of promising Lainie the world on their last Mardi Gras together, and woke up wondering where she was.

There was only one real rule that mattered in war, and that was never for a second forget the constant danger you are in. Forgetting could get you killed. Even during a pickup basketball game on base, on a hot windy day.

HUNT'S T-SHIRT WAS drenched with sweat and stuck to his body. Because of his long arms and ability for high leaps, he'd just blocked a shot from a gunner they called Rat. Rat had retrieved his own rebound and was dribbling back out for a long shot.

Preacher was on Hunt's team. He saw Rat dribbling out, and when he turned to make a long shot, Preacher came running up behind him to steal the ball.

Hunt saw the glee on Preacher's face. Then someone else was shouting at Rat, "Behind you! Behind you!" when all expression on Preacher's face disappeared.

It was the bullet hole in Preacher's forehead that sent Hunt running toward him in a crouch, but he never made it. The second shot fired hit Hunt in the back. The blood from Preacher's head wound was already soaking into the sand as Hunt dropped. He heard T-Bone shouting, "Gator's down," saw Rat running for his weapon, and then somebody turned out the lights.

HE WOKE UP in the ICU of a Level 1 medical unit, with an Army nurse standing over him.

"Welcome back, soldier. Surgery went well. The shot nicked a rib, exited out your side and missed all your vital organs."

Hunt grunted, then closed his eyes.

"You kept saying the name 'Lainie,' over and over. You don't have any next of kin listed. Would you like us to notify her?"

A tear rolled out from under his eyelid. "Don't know where she is. She's lost…like me," Hunt said, and fell back under the drugs.

He learned later they'd taken out the sniper up on the rim of a surrounding mountain, but Preacher was still dead. There would be no more Bible verses as he drew a bad hand at poker. No more preaching in Hunt's ear when they flew. Preacher's war was over, and Hunt's was on hold. He spent two weeks off duty before he was cleared again to fly.

The next time Hunt went up, it was with another pilot, with the call sign, T-Bone. Their missions were successful, but Hunt missed the Bible verses in his ear.

After that, life became a blur. Their company was moved so many times he lost count. They'd get sent stateside only long enough to get their bearings before they'd be deployed to another place of unrest.

Being a chopper pilot meant he owed ten years of his life to the Army, but he often wondered what would happen if he didn't make it to ten. Who would pay that debt for him if he died?

THE FIRST FIVE years of Hunt's service flew past, but the last five felt like forever. On base, it didn't matter so much not getting mail, because they had their own housing. But when they were deployed, mail mattered, and he never received letters or any packages from home, even though the other guys who did always shared.

T-Bone's wife sent gummy bears and Werther's caramels.

Rat's mother sent the best ginger snaps on the planet, and Roadrunner's wife often mailed them huge bags of flavored popcorn.

A pilot they called Memphis got chocolate fudge and

divinity on every holiday, and they fought over the last pieces and laughed.

Cowboy, who was Memphis's gunner, got boxes of homemade beef jerky—a highly sought-after commodity they used for money in their poker games.

Hunt was the odd man out with nothing to share.

WHEN WORD BEGAN to spread that "Gator" was being discharged, his buddies were all in shock. Even Hunt's commanding officer was rendered speechless by the request. He'd assumed Gator would retire out of the Army, but there was no dissuading him, and he accepted the soldier's rights without questioning his reasons.

"Warrant Officer Gray, I have to say, I am sorry to see you go. You have been a huge asset. I hope you find what you're looking for," he said. "I'll put your papers through."

"Thank you, sir," Hunt said, saluted, and then left.

WHEN THE DAY of Hunt's discharge finally rolled around, he was at his quarters on base, packing to leave. He'd left the boy he'd been somewhere back in Louisiana, and the Army had turned what was left of him into a lean soldier with a rock-hard, war-weary body.

Never had he looked more like the old sepia photograph of his great-grandfather than he did now. Crow-black hair. Skin burned brown by desert sun. The beginnings of tiny crow's-feet at the corners of ice blue eyes. A sharp edge to his jaw, and not an ounce of body fat left on him.

He was emotionally burned out.

Over.

Done.

He'd been a part of death and destruction in a way no human should ever face. But war did that, and there was no way around it except to wade through it and ask God for the forgiveness he wasn't able to give himself.

The men he'd flown with and fought with knew he was leaving, and had gathered at his quarters to watch him pack. Their normal chatter was absent. They still couldn't reconcile the fact of never seeing him again.

He knew them by their call signs better than he did their given names. T-Bone. Rat. Roadrunner. Memphis. Cowboy. Galahad. Duke. Sundown. Chili Dog. Tulsa. Cherokee. They'd flown together. Lived together. Bled together.

"You're gonna be a hard act to follow," Rat said.

Gator was a legend among his peers, but in all the years they'd been together, they were beginning to realize they only knew the soldier. They knew nothing about the man.

Roadrunner still couldn't believe he was leaving. "So, Gator, where are you headed?"

Hunt kept shoving socks into his duffel bag without looking up. "Flagstaff. Got a job flying choppers for a charter service."

Rat frowned. "That's a long way from Louisiana. I kinda thought you'd be headed home to family."

Hunt paused, and this time he looked up and began carefully scanning their faces, imprinting the moment forever in his memory.

"This place was home. You are my family. Don't go and get yourselves killed," he said, then shouldered his duffel bag and walked out, with them following behind him.

A soldier and a Humvee were waiting for him. He tossed his bags in the back, crawled into the passenger seat and never looked back as they drove away.

Rat had a lump in his throat and a knot in his belly. It felt like losing a brother. "Dammit. Somebody slap me. I have a sudden urge to cry."

Roadrunner cleared his throat and swiped at his eyes. "He never did get over losing Preacher."

Rat shook his head. "I think he lost someone who mattered more, long before he came here."

HUNT SPENT HIS first night as a civilian in a hotel in nearby Fayetteville. He had a flight out to Flagstaff the next morning, and after he got to his room, he checked in with Pete Randolph, the man who would be his new boss.

"Hey, Hunt. Where are you?" Pete asked.

"Still in North Carolina. I have a flight out tomorrow. I'll be in Flagstaff sometime late afternoon."

"Awesome! We're really looking forward to you joining the crew, but take time to find living quarters. Tend to whatever business you need to do, and then give me a call when you've settled, and I'll show you around."

"Thanks, Pete. I appreciate this."

"Hey, I'm the one who got lucky. You're the most highly trained chopper pilot I've ever hired. Even with all my years in the air, you've got me beat. You flew Longbows, man. An Apache pilot is an ace in my book."

"Ex-Apache pilot. I like flying, but I can do without being shot at. I'll be in touch," he said, then disconnected.

HUNT WAS AT the airport early the next morning. He grabbed a sweet roll and a coffee on his way to his gate, and without thinking, began searching the faces of every approaching female in the concourse, while ignoring the looks women were giving him.

The aviator sunglasses he wore had a twofold purpose. Wearing them to hide his eyes was like wearing a mask, as well as using them for blocking out the sun. He didn't have civilian clothes that fit anymore, and was wearing dark charcoal tactical pants and a plain gray T-shirt beneath his flight jacket. The shirt clung to his abs like a lover, giving a hint of the dog tags beneath it.

His boots were old, but polished. He was wearing a baseball cap with an Army star insignia, and his black leather flight jacket with an official Army patch on the back, and an Apache chopper patch on his sleeve.

He knew the odds of seeing Lainie again were infinitesimal, but through all the times he thought he would die in a country not his own, luck had been with him. It stood to reason he could get lucky again.

When he reached the gate, he stood near a window to use the sill for a table, and set his coffee on it while he ate. It was the first time in years that the choices he was making were all his own. The weight of duty had been shed, and he felt lighter. If he wanted, he could search for Lainie now. But there was a part of him afraid to find out where she was. He didn't want to know if she'd married someone else. He couldn't bear the thought of her sleeping in someone else's arms. So, he let the thought fade, and decided to let fate play the hand for him.

When they began boarding, he fell in line, and once

on the plane quickly took his seat. It felt strange being in a regular passenger plane, but he wasn't flying over hostile territory anymore, and after the plane was in the air, he stretched his legs and put the cap in his lap.

A flight attendant came by later and quietly whispered, "Thank you for your service," as she handed him a beverage.

He grasped the cup and nodded.

And elderly man in the opposite aisle had already seen the patches on Hunt's jacket, and leaned across the aisle.

"Active duty?" he asked.

Hunt shook his head. "Not anymore."

"Ah…headed home, then," the man said.

"I'm already home," Hunt said. "Just looking for a place to be," then finished his beverage, set the empty cup on the tray table and closed his eyes.

After that, nobody bothered him. He changed planes in Atlanta, and then had a straight flight to Flagstaff from there. By the time he landed, it was late afternoon. He caught a cab to the hotel where he'd made a reservation, and as soon as he had checked in and dumped his stuff in his room, he went down to the dining room and ordered steak with all the trimmings, and sweet tea. It wasn't southern sweet, but it suited him. Afterward, he went straight back to his room to shower and shave, then kicked back in bed with the intent of watching a movie, and fell asleep within minutes.

And he dreamed.

Lainie was lying beneath him, her arms locked around his neck. There were tears in her eyes, and her lips were slightly parted, as if trying to catch her breath. They'd both been scared when they laid down. She'd never had sex. He'd never made love to a virgin. He was fully erect and protected, and she was willing, but this was a hell of a responsibility he didn't want to flub.

"I love you, Lainie, but don't know how to keep from hurting you," he whispered.

"I know that, but I love you, too, and you're worth it," she said, and held her breath as he moved between her legs, and then slipped inside her, felt the barrier and pushed.

Quick tears came with a gasp, and then he began to move, and the pain was gone. She looked up into the face above her, and then wrapped her arms around his neck and closed her eyes. It felt good. It felt right. And it kept getting better. She didn't know what a climax was until it hit, and then she lost her mind.

The blood rush was still rolling through when Hunt raised up and began searching her face, afraid of what she'd think. How she'd feel.

"Did it hurt you, darlin'?"

"Only for a second," she said. "The rest was magic."

His hands were in her hair as he leaned down and kissed her.

"I have dreamed of what this would be like, to make love to you. It was perfect. You're perfect."

Her gaze was locked upon his face. He had that raptor look in his eyes. Like he'd just caught the prey he'd been after, and claimed it. It was the side of him that turned him into a machine on the football field. That fight or die mindset. She loved it and she loved him.

"Hunter James Gray, you are my first love. My last love. My only love. It will always be you."

"God, Lainie. I don't know what I did to deserve you, but I love you so much I ache from it," he whispered, then moved from her, and stretched out beside her instead.

Silence filled the moments as they nestled in each other's arms, but it was Lainie who broke the silence, and her voice was shaking when she spoke.

"If I ever get lost from you, Hunt, don't quit me. It will never be my choice."

He knew where that was coming from. Their fathers' war.

"If they cause trouble, I'll find a way to save you. I promise," he said.

"I promise... I promise... I promise."

HUNT WOKE UP saying the words. "I promise. I promise."

The moment he heard his voice, the old regret rolled through him, but today he was starting over. He threw back the covers and headed for the shower again. He had a thousand things to do today, and finding a place to live was first on the list.

WITHIN A WEEK, Hunt signed a lease on a 900 square foot, two-bedroom, one-bath house on the outskirts of Flagstaff. He just spent the last ten years of his life within an army, responding to orders shouted, the constant chatter of conversation, and when deployed, a multitude of snoring. He needed peace and privacy. He was lost, and looking for the man he would be without the boots and uniforms.

With a new address to his name, he then contacted the lawyer back in New Orleans to have his personal papers sent. He didn't know if his parents still lived where they had, or if they were even still alive, and didn't care. They were part of what broke him.

The job he'd taken with Randolph Tours and Charters was perfect. Nothing was asked of him but to ferry people from one place to another. Wherever he went, he was always home by evening. The churning waters of his life were beginning to calm. He was almost twenty-nine years old, and most days, he felt fifty, but life went on, taking him with it.

SIX HUNDRED SEVENTY-SEVEN miles north, Lainie Mayes was leaving home in a downpour on her way to work at Denver Health Center. She'd long ago switched her studies from nursing to X-ray and radiology, then on to becoming Certified in Radiologic Technology. She was coming up on her ninth year at the facility, and was as satisfied with her path in life as she knew how to be. There was a hole in her heart, and a tear in her soul, but she was still standing. She glanced back at the house as she was driving away.

It was her refuge. The place where she could unload frustrations and tears in the privacy of her own home, and she bought it the second year after she received her CRT certification.

THE THREE-BEDROOM BRICK, two bath house had been a fixer-upper when she took possession, and the first thing she did was hire a contractor to remodel and update it to her style.

The first thing she changed were the old red bricks. She had them painted a soft, eggshell white, then re-painted the shutters sage green. The extra-wide door was stripped down to the wood, and refinished in a cherrywood stain to match the fireplace mantel in the living room.

And when the exterior was finished, the contractor began restructuring the interior, taking down walls, re-modeling the entire kitchen, retiling the fireplace and the bathrooms, adding a stand-up shower in the en suite, and a soaker tub instead of the old Jacuzzi. She finished all the walls in white, and used furniture and decor to add color.

The fireplace had been converted to gas logs, which suited her, and she also kept the massive cherrywood mantel and retiled the surround. It was her favorite fea-ture in the house. Not only was it striking, but useful in offsetting the harsh Denver winters.

One day not long after she moved, she picked up a child-size rocking chair at a tag sale. When she got home, she set it beside the hearth, then went into her bedroom to get her old teddy bear and carried it back to the fire-place.

She gave the soft, floppy bear a gentle hug. "My trea-sures forever," she whispered, then set it down in the rocker and stepped back to get a better view.

After all these years, the bear's floppy head had begun to tilt the slightest bit to the right, like it was waiting to hear another secret. Without Hunt in her life, she'd given them all to his bear.

She turned the smallest bedroom into an office, and lined an entire wall with bookshelves, and through the ensuing years, filled them with books. On her days off when the weather was dreary, she puttered around her kitchen, trying new recipes and baking, and when the weather was good, she hiked the trails in the surrounding mountains.

The day she finally moved in, she said a little prayer, thanking her grandmother's generosity in leaving her that trust, and settled in like a little hen in a nest. She liked her job, and had long since mastered driving in snow. In short, Denver had become her home.

She'd framed Hunt's last text message to her, and hung it over the headboard of her bed as a talisman against bad dreams and lonely nights. But it didn't stop the longing. Time had not eased her broken heart.

She was barely twenty when she first began working at the hospital; she'd had to go through the gamut of being the new, single woman on the job. Doctors, interns, coworkers, even patients hit on her, and her friends kept trying to fix her up with dates, until they realized it was futile. They didn't know her story, but it was apparent having a partner of any kind was not on her radar.

Sometimes she'd hang out with friends, but only as part of a group, and wherever she went, she arrived alone and left the same way. She didn't want another man holding her. Kissing her. Making love to her. She'd had the best. And if she couldn't have Hunt, she chose no one at all.

THE RAIN WAS still pouring as Lainie pulled into the employee parking lot, but she'd come prepared. She had a raincoat over her clothes, and an umbrella over her head as she got out running. Once inside, she headed to her locker, stowed her things, grabbed the lanyard with her ID and pass card and put it around her neck. After a quick check of her pockets to make sure she had everything she needed, she locked her locker and went to check the schedule.

Soon, she was on the job, readying a thirtysomething woman for X-rays. After that, it was a succession of patients, and the morning passed. When there was a break in her schedule, she went down to the cafeteria to grab some lunch, and saw some friends eating at a table, and headed over.

"Got room for one more?" she asked.

A little blonde named Charis Colby waved a French fry in the air. "Sit by me," she said. "I need positive vibes. I just weighed myself this morning and it's not looking good for that wedding dress I'm soon going to need."

Lainie smiled at the comment and the French fry as she sat. "So, you've finally set a date, have you?"

Charis rolled her eyes. "I have six months to pull a wedding together. My mother is in hysterics. You'd think she was the one getting married."

They laughed in sympathy, and then picked up the conversation, most of which was hospital gossip, as they ate. Lainie kept an eye on the time and was just about finished when she noticed a heavyset man in scrubs approaching the table with a food tray. He was a bald, thirtysomething man with broad shoulders, and a mat of thick brown hair on his arms, but it was the look on his face that alerted every ounce of self-preservation within her. To her dismay, he stopped at their table. Before she could leave, Charis was introducing her.

"Hey Lainie, this is Justin Randall…a new nurse on our floor. Justin, this is Lainie Mayes. She's in radiology."

"Lainie, it's a pleasure to meet you," he said.

Lainie nodded politely. "You, too. Welcome to Denver Health. Sorry, but I've gotta run. Later, y'all."

She picked up her tray as she went, sorted the dirty dishes and silverware at the station, and left the cafeteria. She didn't have to look back to know he was still watching her. She could feel it, and it gave her the creeps.

Justin frowned as he watched her go, then put down his tray and sat in the chair she'd just vacated. He took note of the warm leather still holding the shape of her backside, and let dirty thoughts roll through his head as he took his first bite.

Her day got crazy, and toward the end of her shift, she wound up down in ER with a portable X-ray, trying to get film on an unconscious child who'd been pulled from a wreck. By the time she headed home for the evening, she'd forgotten Justin Randall even existed.

But Justin Randall hadn't forgotten her. She was exactly his type. Her auburn hair fit into the category of redheads. She was average height, busty and lean, and by the time his lunch with his coworkers was over, he now knew she was single, too. All he had to do was bide his time. She given off all kinds of "don't touch" vibes, but he didn't care. He liked a good fight.

He picked up a pizza and a six-pack of beer on his way home, and settled in to watch the sports channel, while Lainie was in her oversize soaker tub on the other side of the city, up to her neck in lavender-scented bubbles.

THE ARRIVAL OF Justin Randall began to change Lainie's routine at work. He appeared at random times, in random places where she was working, and at first, she thought little of it. But then it dawned on her that while she moved around within the floors and halls of the hospital according to what her job required, his job did not. He was a nurse on an assigned floor, and yet there he'd be, out of place and in her face.

As the months passed, he began upping his approach, trying to include her in group lunches, asking her to go bowling, to take a ride, to have coffee, and every time, she turned him down. Some days, she made excuses. Other days it was a flat no.

But on this morning when she saw him coming, it was too late to make an escape, and all of a sudden, he was in her face.

"Lainie! You're looking great today! How about a drink after work? I know this place with great bar food and even better drinks."

"Thanks, but I have other plans. Gotta go. They're waiting for me," she said, and kept walking.

Even though he was talking to her back now, he still persisted. "Maybe another time," he called out, and frowned when she didn't respond.

Before the week was out, he'd blindsided her two more times—appearing out of nowhere. All she could think was that he had to be following her. Why wasn't he on his floor?

Finally, she cornered Charis midweek in the cafeteria. Charis was alone at the table, and Lainie immediately sat down.

"Charis, isn't Justin Randall assigned to your floor?"

Charis nodded. "Yes, why?"

Lainie leaned closer and lowered her voice. "Everywhere I go, no matter what floor I'm on, there he is. It's been going on for months. He just appears out of nowhere, asking me out. I make excuses but he doesn't quit. He's in my face. He's in my personal space. And he creeps me out."

Charis frowned. "How long has this been happening?"

"Since almost from the time you introduced us. He's giving out stalker vibes like you wouldn't believe, and you know me. I don't flirt. I'm not sending out any vibes that could be misconstrued."

Charis's frown deepened. "Oh, honey, I'm so sorry. I'll put a bug in the supervisor's ear, and let her know he's not on the job like he's supposed to be. Other than that, I don't know what else to do."

Lainie's shoulders slumped. "Thanks. I've never experienced anything remotely close to this, and it's getting scary. These are the times when I wish to God I still had Hunter Gray in my life," she said, and then went quiet, shocked that she'd actually spoken out loud.

Charis stilled. This was the first time any of them had ever heard her mention a man.

"So, he's the reason you don't date?" she asked.

Lainie nodded.

"I'm so sorry. What happened?"

"Our fathers happened. They were stepbrothers who hated each other, and Hunt and I committed an unpardonable sin. We fell in love. Life happened. And we lost each other. I don't know where he is. I don't even know if he's still alive in the world…if he even lived to become a man, but he was my everything. He stood between me and our fathers' hate until they broke me, and when that happened, I think it broke him, too."

Charis was horrified. "Here I am all gushing about my happy life and pending marriage, and you're living with this. I'm so sorry. That's the saddest thing I think I've ever heard."

Lainie shrugged. "It is what it is. Look, I would appreciate you keeping this to yourself. Hospital gossip is deadly. I don't want this to be my identity because it's not. That was me at eighteen. I'm neither broken nor helpless. All I want is Justin Randall to leave me the hell alone."

Charis nodded. "I promise. And I'll talk to our supervisor, too."

"As long as he doesn't find out that I'm the one who ratted him out, it should be fine," Lainie said, but those were famous last words.

The next day, Lainie clocked in, locked up her things and was on her way out of the break room when Justin walked up behind her.

"Hey Lainie!" he said, and gripped her shoulder hard enough it physically stopped her in her tracks.

She jerked, then shoved his hand away. "What the hell, Justin? You scared me half to death! Don't sneak up on people like that, okay?"

She knew the minute she said it that he was angry, because his eyes narrowed, and the smile on his face turned into a thin-lipped grimace.

"Sorry! Didn't know you were so touchy. I know you're off tomorrow, and so am I. I thought it would be fun to—"

Lainie held up her hand. "Justin, just stop. I'm not interested in dating anyone. Period. I don't intend to hurt your feelings, but let's not have this conversation again, okay? Now, I have to hurry, and that's not an excuse. I'm doing MRIs all day today, and we don't keep people waiting."

"Yeah, sure. No problem. I understand," he said, and walked off.

Lainie breathed a quick sigh of relief, thinking he'd finally gotten the message, and hurried up the hall.

Her first patient, a fortysomething woman named Renee Reilly, was already in tears from the fear of the test itself, when Lainie arrived, but she quickly launched into patient mode and began talking her down.

"Hi, Renee, I'm Lainie, your MRI technician. We're doing an open MRI with contrast today, right?"

Renee nodded. "My doctor explained the process. I'm just scared."

"That's fair, and I certainly understand. We can talk while I start your IV so we can begin the drip for the contrast."

"Yes, okay," Renee said, and closed her eyes as the needle went in.

"There we go," Lainie said, as she taped it down, and started the drip. "This will take about twenty minutes or so to finish. Are you cold? I can get you a blanket."

"A blanket would be good," Renee said.

Lainie got a fresh one from the warmer and tucked it around her. "I'm going to be just inside the lab here getting things ready. I'll check back with you in a few minutes."

Renee stifled a sob. "I have cancer. I just know it. The women on my side of the family all die from it. I have three children still at home. They're going to grow up without me," she wailed.

Lainie paused, then pulled up a chair and sat down. "I've been at this job in one capacity or another for almost nine years now, and if there's one thing I've learned about medicine, it is that we never assume anything, okay? The only man I ever loved had a saying that always made me laugh. 'Darlin'." She paused and smiled. "He always called me darlin'. Anyway, he would say, 'Darlin', you never want to borrow trouble. The only safe thing to borrow is eggs and butter.'"

Renee smiled through tears. "Sounds like a wonderful guy."

"The best," Lainie said. "Now, let's just get through this test, and then you go home and take your kids out for pizza tonight. I believe in using every day to make memories. Nobody knows what their tomorrow will bring. I don't know what awaits me, any more than your doctor knows what awaits him. One day at a time, honey. One day at a time. How about some music while you wait?" she asked.

Renee squeezed Lainie's hand. "Yes, please, and thank you for that."

"Absolutely," Lainie said. "What kind of music do you like?"

"Music from the '80s."

"You got it," Lainie said, slipped headphones on her, pulled up the proper link and started it playing.

When Renee gave her a thumbs-up and closed her eyes, Lainie slipped into the control area, and began checking the orders to confirm the imaging required for the test.

When it finally came time for Renee to be moved into the open MRI, she was calm enough to follow all the directions. It would be an hour-long process of immobility, flat on her back, with the thump and pulse of the machine around her upper body being drowned out by Bon Jovi singing in her ears.

When the test was finally over, Lainie helped Renee out of the machine and then helped her sit up. "Everything okay? Are you dizzy sitting up now?"

"No, I feel fine," Renee said.

"Good. Now, what are you doing this evening?" Lainie asked.

Renee grinned. "Having pizza with the family at Famous Pizza and Subs."

"Yum! Eat a slice for me!"

"Count on it," Renee said, "and thank you."

Lainie helped her into a wheelchair, and signaled for the waiting orderly to take her out.

Before her day was over, she'd done three more MRIs, and was emotionally exhausted. Dealing with patients' stress was always more complicated than the actual act of her job. She knew the job and did it well. She just never knew what drama, if any, the next patient might bring.

She finally clocked out and was walking across the parking lot when she saw Charis, and waved.

"See you tomorrow!" Charis called.

"My day off! I'm hiking Beaver Brook Trail tomorrow!"

Charis rolled her eyes. "Better you than me. Some of us are going to Adelitas tomorrow evening for drinks and tacos. Seven o'clock. You're invited!"

"Deal!" Lainie said. "See you there!"

"Yay!" Charis said and did a little two-step as she got in her car and drove away.

Lainie envied Charis's ebullience as she was driving away, unaware Justin Randall had overheard everything, including her hiking destination.

Chapter Three

Even though it was her day off, Lainie had set the alarm the night before. She wanted to be on the trail just after sunrise. It was her favorite time of day to begin a hike. The air was still cool, and she'd be on her way back down by the time the day was heating up.

She'd packed her backpack the night before with protein bars, snack packs, first aid, bear spray and a hunting knife. All she had to add were water bottles, and did so before zipping it up.

After checking the weather report for the day, she opted for long pants, sneakers, thick socks, a long-sleeve T-shirt and a flannel shirt to use as a jacket. She had her hiking pole, and a compass, a cell phone, and a charger stick in her pack, just in case.

She put her long hair in a ponytail at the back of her neck, and tied a bandanna around her forehead. Her sunglasses were already in the car, and after a quick breakfast, she headed out the door.

Traffic was already moving at a steady pace as she wound her way west out of Denver and into the foothills toward her chosen hiking path. She liked the Beaver Brook Trail for a number of reasons. The likelihood of running into a lot of other hikers at this time of morning on a weekday was slim, and that suited her.

She was already anticipating the hike as she arrived at the parking area below the trailhead. Pleased that there were no other vehicles around, she got out, dropped the car keys in her pocket, shouldered her backpack, reached for her hiking pole and started up the trail.

JUSTIN RANDALL HAD no idea what time of day Lainie liked to hike, but he was betting it was early. He had the GPS in his phone already set, and was hoping to beat her there, find a secluded place to park and wait for her to arrive. As he drove across town, he quickly learned it was cooler than he'd expected, and was wishing he'd worn long pants instead of hiking shorts. But he would warm up as he hiked, and was making good time through traffic when the truck in front of him blew through a red light.

It hit two cars making opposite turns in the intersection, which threw them into other cars, and by the time the crashing and skidding was over, four cars, a police car, a delivery van and the truck were in a tangled mess at the four-way light.

Traffic came to a halt. There was no way to back up, and no way to move forward. Justin was cursing his luck as police and emergency vehicles began arriving, but there was nothing to do but wait. It took almost an hour before a lane had been cleared for traffic to detour on a nearby street. He had to reset his GPS to get where he was headed from another direction, and by the time he reached the trailhead, the one positive of his morning was that her car was the only one in the parking lot. He laid his hand on the hood, but it was already cool, which meant she'd been gone for some time.

He didn't know if the trail forked, and if it did, which way she would go. He was angry and frustrated, but changing his plan never occurred to him. He was hell-bent on one destination, and that was to get between her legs. So, he shouldered his pack and took off up the trail at a trot.

A CARDINAL WAS flitting from tree to tree along the path Lainie was on, and after a while, she decided it was following her. Delighted, she began talking to it as she went, fantasizing about how and why it was happening.

"I see you...flying from tree to tree along my path. Have we met before? You'll have to excuse me. I'm terrible with names."

A flash of red shot across her line of vision about twenty feet in front of her, and landed on a low-hanging branch. It was the cardinal. She watched as it turned its head one way, and then the other, before dropping to the ground below, where it promptly gobbled up a bug.

"The mighty hunter scores!" she said, as the bird flew back into the tree.

She glanced at the sun, guessing it must be nearing 10:00 a.m. by now, and paused to take a drink.

The cardinal flew off as she began moving again, and for a while, she thought he'd finally flown away. It wasn't until the bird suddenly reappeared that she paused, curious as to what it was doing.

It was that pause that saved her.

In that moment of silence, she heard footsteps on the trail behind her and glanced over her shoulder, expecting another hiker. There was a man behind her, hoofing it up the trail at an unusually hasty pace, but when she saw his face, a wave of panic rolled through her.

Justin Randall!

She shouted at him, angry that he'd made her afraid. "Justin! What the hell are you playing at? There are laws against stalking, and I've made myself perfectly clear."

Justin began smiling and waving his hands. "Lainie! Wait! It's not what you think!" Then began moving faster, to get to her before she bolted.

She'd already dropped her backpack and was fumbling for the bear spray when he started running. Her hands were shaking as she popped the top, and got one good spray toward his face, before he knocked it out of her hand.

He had closed his eyes at the last minute, but the spray still went up his nose, and all of a sudden, the inside of his nose was on fire and his throat was swelling. When his eyes began to burn and his vision blur, he swung a fist at her face. One punch landed on her cheekbone below her eye, and another missed her face and hit the side of her neck.

And just like that, Lainie was back in her bedroom with her father, fighting for her life. She couldn't let Justin Randall knock her out. She had no chance of getting through this alive unless she stayed conscious.

She was still in a panic when he grabbed her by her arms and took her down, straddling her lower body and pinning her arms above her head.

But Lainie was fighting for her life, kicking and thrashing beneath him, and in one brief moment when he let go of her hands to rip at her clothes, she stabbed her fingernails into his face, and raked them all the way down his cheek and neck, plowing furrows into his flesh, then began kicking and scratching at his neck and arms until her hand was slick with his blood.

"You bitch," he roared, and then threw back his head and laughed. "I knew you'd like it rough!"

She dug her fingers into the ground, intent on throwing dirt in his eyes, and felt a softball-size rock beneath her palm instead. She grabbed it without hesitation and swung it at his head. The crack when it hit was the sound of sticks breaking.

He grunted and fell backward, stunned by the blow. She rolled to her knees, grabbed the same rock with both hands and smashed it down onto his mouth and nose. Blood spurted from his lips, as he spit out a tooth to keep from swallowing it. He had both hands on his face, rolling and moaning, as Lainie leaped to her feet and started running.

She went flying down the trail, leaving everything behind her but the car keys in her pocket, knowing she had to outrun him to survive, and run she did, until her side was aching and every breath she took was like swallowing fire.

She didn't know he was behind her until she began hearing curses and shouts. She looked over her shoulder in horror. He was covered in blood, carrying both backpacks and her hiking pole, and running like a man possessed about a hundred yards behind her.

Hope sank. "God help me," she mumbled, and ran faster.

It wasn't until she was started down a steep drop on the path that she realized she was in what hikers called "the blind spot."

She couldn't see him when she looked back, which meant he couldn't see her either. And it was becoming all too clear that he was going to catch her before she ever got to her car. At that moment, she remembered something Hunt used to say.

When faced with a hard decision, do the unexpected.

So, she faked her death.

She yanked off her sneakers, then threw one partway down the slope along with her flannel shirt, and left the other one in the path. Then she dropped and rolled in the trail to make it look like she had a bad fall and rolled off into the canyon below.

Still in her sock feet, she leaped across the path on the other side and ran deep into the trees and brush before pausing to get her bearings. She couldn't keep going down, because that's where he was going, so she hunkered down and began moving in a crouch back up the mountain, and never looked back.

THE LAST THING Justin expected to see was one of Lainie's sneakers on the trail, and then he saw where she fell and looked over the slope, saw her flannel shirt first, and then the other shoe.

Holy shit. The bitch fell off the mountain.

He let out a sigh of relief, and then realized he was still carrying her things. The first thing he did was wipe his prints off her hiking pole before he tossed it down the slope, and then he slung her backpack down with it.

His whole face was on fire. He could feel the furrows she'd left on his face and knew he had to get them treated, but he stopped long enough to use a bottle of his drinking water to wash off what he could of blood and bear spray.

He was confident animals would destroy her body, but his DNA was all over her clothes and backpack, so he began concocting an alibi on his way to his car.

They'd gone hiking together and were surprised by a bear. He was trying to protect her when the bear knocked them both down. He sprayed the bear, got caught in some of the blowback, and was unaware that she'd been knocked over the side of the mountain until after the bear ran away.

Then, he sat in his car and watched TikTok videos until his phone went dead, and his wounds wouldn't be fresh, before driving himself to the nearest emergency room. He staggered in, claiming he'd been knocked unconscious after a bear attack, that his hiking partner was missing, and he'd found a shoe in the path and seen some of her gear on the downslope. His best guess was that she'd fallen off the path into a canyon, but he was too weak to search on his own, and when he got to his car, his phone was dead, so he drove himself to the ER.

Within the hour, both the local police and the Denver Park Rangers were in ER taking his statement, while a doctor and nurse continued to clean up his wounds. They put four staples in his head wound, reset his broken nose and told him to see his dentist, and to drink his meals through straws for the next couple of weeks.

A nurse was swabbing out the scratches as he continued to answer questions, but she wasn't buying the whole story. So, while the police were still questioning Justin, she signaled for the doctor to come out into the hall.

"What's wrong?" he asked.

"Those scratches on his face and neck don't look like bear scratches. They look like fingernail scratches. And he has them on his wrists and neck, and upper arms, too. If his hiking partner is missing, he might be the reason why."

The doctor frowned and went back into the exam room. "Mr. Randall, I want to take another look at the wounds on your face to make sure we've gotten out all of the debris."

Justin didn't say anything, but he was worried. When the cops began whispering between themselves, and then one of them requested the wounds be swabbed for DNA, then took possession of all of the swabs they'd used to clean the scratches the first time, he knew they weren't buying all of his story. But since it was the only one he had, he was sticking to it.

LAINIE'S SIDE WAS ACHING. She was exhausted and stumbling, and out of breath. It felt like she'd been running forever. There was an outcrop of rocks in an open space just ahead, and her focus was just getting to the patch of shade beneath it when she stumbled again, and fell forward before she had time to catch herself. Her head hit the side of the outcrop as she went down, and she was unconscious before she landed.

It was late evening before she woke up with dirt in her mouth and a huge cut on her lip. Her head was one solid ache, and when she moved, everything spun around her. As she rolled over to sit up, something ran down the side of her face. She thought it was sweat and gave it a swipe, only to have her hand come away covered in blood.

"No, no, no," she whispered, and put her head between her knees to keep from passing out.

She couldn't figure out where she was, or what had happened, and began looking around for her backpack, and that's when she remembered. The last time she'd seen it, Justin Randall had it. She groaned, remembering now that she'd tried to throw him off her trail by pretending that she had fallen into the canyon. But what if he was still out there looking for her? What was she supposed to do?

Her hands were trembling as she took the bandanna off her forehead, refolded it and tied it over the bleeding cut, then thought about trying to get up. But when she looked down and saw bear tracks in the dirt all around where she was sitting, she was on her feet before she thought. The motion was too fast, and she nearly went down again.

Her best guess was that she had a concussion, and steadied herself against the outcrop until the world stopped spinning. After that, she took a closer look at the tracks. She couldn't decide if they were old tracks, or if a bear had sniffed around her while she was unconscious, then wandered off. The thought was terrifying, and her biggest fear now became the bear. What if it came back looking for her?

Without thinking, she charged off, staggering and stumbling as she went, until the sun began going down, taking warmth with it. Her head was pounding, and she needed a place out of the wind for the night, and began keeping an eye out as she walked. When she came upon a ledge of rocks with just enough space beneath to crawl under, she stopped. The possibility of a snake crawling up beside her in the night was real, so she began gathering dry brush and small branches, then crawled beneath the ledge and pulled the branches in all around her.

She wanted a drink of water so bad she could almost taste it, and everything hurt, and she was so cold, but exhaustion overwhelmed fear. She curled up, closed her eyes and dreamed.

SHE WAS RUNNING and then she was driving, and then she was walking, and every time she saw a stranger she'd stop and ask, "Have you seen Hunter? Have you seen my man?" And every time, they would shake their heads and leave her standing.

Then the dream morphed, and she was in a boat on a river, and fog was so thick she couldn't see the shore. The boat had no motor or oars, and she was screaming, "Help me! Help me!" but to no avail.

Then from a distance, she heard a voice. She knew that voice, and stood up in the boat and began to scream. "Help, Hunter! Help. I'm here!" But the boat kept floating farther and farther away, until the world around her was silent once more.

WHEN SEVEN O'CLOCK came and went at Adelitas restaurant and Lainie still wasn't there, Charis called her. The call went to voice mail. Thirty minutes later, she sent a text that wasn't answered, and then another one, and by the time the evening was over, and Charis was headed home, she was still worried enough to drive by Lainie's house. Yet, after she got there, she couldn't tell if the car was in the garage. But her lights were out, so she drove home, telling herself everything was surely okay, convincing herself that when she saw Lainie tomorrow, she would have a logical explanation.

WHEN LAINIE WOKE up again, it was morning, and a raccoon was staring at her through the brush she'd pulled in around her. As soon as she opened her eyes, it waddled away.

The moment she took a breath, she knew something was wrong. It hurt to breathe, and her skin felt hot. When she felt her head wound, her fingers came away bloody. This meant the cut was still seeping blood through the bandanna, and now she had a fever. It was all she could do to crawl out from beneath the ledge, and the only thing on her mind was finding water. There hadn't been any behind her, so up she went.

She was still sad from the dream. And it took everything she had to put one foot in front of the other, but she was lost. Not dead. Surely someone would miss her at work. Charis knew where she'd gone. She had to believe someone would find her. She just needed to be found before she was past help.

WHEN LAINIE DIDN'T show up for work, Charis panicked and went straight to Jennifer Wilson, Lainie's boss.

"Have you talked to Lainie? Has she called in?"

"No, and it's not like her to miss work without calling," Jennifer said.

"She went hiking yesterday and was supposed to meet us for dinner last night, but never showed. I drove by her house on my way home, but all the lights were off, and I couldn't tell if her car was in the garage or not. Please, call the police and ask them to do a welfare check. Something's wrong! I just know it!"

Jennifer made the call, but the moment she mentioned Lainie Mayes's name, she got the shock of her life and quickly put the call on speaker so Charis could hear the officer's reply.

"I'm sorry, ma'am, but that person has already been reported missing by her hiking partner last night. He showed up in an ER with severe wounds. He said he and Miss Mayes were hiking together when they were attacked by a bear. He was injured, but managed to spray it in the face with bear repellant before being knocked unconscious. When he came to, she was missing. He found one of her shoes on the path, and saw some of her other belongings on the slope down into the canyon. He drove himself to ER to report the incident. There is already an ongoing search party, and we're still questioning him."

Charis gasped, and then interrupted the officer.

"No, Officer, no! She would never have gone hiking with that man. He's been stalking and harassing her at work for months. If he showed up in an ER with wounds, it wasn't from any bear. I promise it was Lainie, fighting for her life."

There was a moment of silence, and then the officer spoke. "I'm going to need your name and contact information, and we'll be asking you to come to the station to make a statement."

"Anything! I'll do anything for Lainie," Charis said. "Just don't turn that man loose."

The call ended. Charis and Jennifer stared at each other in disbelief.

THE PARK RANGERS were already in search mode. They had Randall's statement about where the attack happened, and followed the path up to the spot. They found a shoe on the path, as he'd stated, and then another shoe and a shirt on the slope, farther down. They also found a hiking stick, but what they didn't find were bear tracks.

After that, they took the search down into the canyon below, expecting to find her, or her body, but the only other thing the searchers found was her backpack hanging from a tree. It was too far away from the other stuff to have fallen with her, and there was no body, and no sign of drag marks or footprints walking away anywhere beneath it.

They were already suspicious of Justin Randall's story, and were now fairly certain of foul play. She'd obviously been attacked on the trail, but not by a bear, and the bigger question was, was she even still on the mountain?

By midafternoon, the local-hiker-gone-missing story was all over the local news, and by evening, the national news had picked it up.

Justin Randall was in his apartment, so sore he could hardly move, and drinking soup from a cup, when there was a knock at the door. He set the cup down and hob-bled to the door.

A detective and four policemen were in the hall.

"Mr. Randall, we need you to come with us," the detective said.

"What the hell? Why?" Justin asked.

"Because your story is full of great big holes, and we need you to come fill those up for us."

Justin was blustering and arguing all the way out the door, and still cursing as they put him in a squad car and drove away.

HUNTER GRAY HAD flown a group of tourists to the South Rim of the Grand Canyon earlier in the day, and he'd just set down to unload them. They were already on their way to the office, and he was doing a final systems check as he shut down. When he finished, he climbed out of the cockpit and started across the tarmac, as the sun was setting behind his back.

He entered the office, signed himself out, and then sat down to wait to talk to Pete before going home. The television on the wall behind him was on, and he wasn't paying much attention to it until he heard a name that stopped his heart. He spun, his gaze immediately fixed on the monitor, and the journalist doing an on-the-spot commentary of what was happening.

"...Lainic Mayes, an employee of Denver Health Center has gone missing. She was last reported to have gone hiking with a friend in the mountains west of the city on Beaver Brook Trail. According to the report, they were attacked by a bear, and in the ensuing drama, she was knocked off the trail and down into a canyon, while the friend was still fighting the bear. He wound up in ER and they are combing the area as we speak. A search has turned up articles of her clothing, and a backpack down in the canyon off the trail, but Miss Mayes's body has yet to be located. Searchers are…"

But it wasn't until they flashed a photo that reality hit. He grunted like he'd been gut punched, and nearly went to his knees, then headed for Pete's office.

Pete was on the phone, a little irked and surprised by Hunt's abrupt entrance, until he saw his face.

"Hunt! What's wrong?"

"Someone I love is lost in the mountains west of Denver. They're searching for her now, and I have to go. I won't be back until I find her."

His eyes widened. "The woman hiker who went missing?"

Hunt nodded. "I'm sorry, but she means everything to me. I have to—"

"Do you need a ride? I can fly you there in the morning," Pete said.

"I can't wait that long. I'm driving up tonight. Thanks, boss," and then he was gone.

As he was driving home, he kept thinking of how close in proximity he'd been to her. He'd been here for months and all the while she was within driving distance. Now, he felt sick that he hadn't searched for her sooner. He couldn't bear the thought of it being too late.

As soon as he got home, he began to focus on what to do first. He needed to pack survival gear, including his SAT phone. He needed to know where she'd been hiking, and where the search site was located, so he did a little online research to see what he could find out. Army life had taught him to never go into a fight unprepared. If she was still alive, he had to accept that he couldn't just go storming into her life as if he still had a right to be there, but he'd made her a promise. If she ever got lost, he would save her. Even if she belonged to someone else now, he still owed her that vow.

BUT HUNT WASN'T the only one in a state of shock about Lainie's fate. Her parents had already heard the same report earlier in the day. They'd had no idea where she was or what she'd been doing since she disappeared, and learning this now was horrifying. Their biggest regret was fearing they were going to be too late to ever speak to her again.

"What do we do?" Greg asked.

Tina was in tears. "We go there. We abandoned her once at her request, but she's not around to ask permission, and I need to know if my daughter is alive or dead."

They caught the last flight out of New Orleans, with a plane change in Dallas. They wouldn't arrive in Denver until after 2:00 a.m., but they didn't care. They just wanted to be on-site.

It was nearing four in the morning by the time they reached the hotel where they'd booked a room. It was too late to sleep, so they showered, changed clothes and went down for an early breakfast before asking the concierge about renting a car.

UNAWARE THAT GREG and Tina Mayes were en route to Denver, Hunt was showering and packing, getting ready to make the drive. It was nearly an eleven-hour trip from Flagstaff to Denver, so he'd be driving all night, but there were things he needed to know. It was just past sundown when he sat down at his laptop and typed her name in the search bar.

Within moments dozens and dozens of links popped up. Surprised by the number of them, he began with the ones in the year she went missing. And to his horror, every paper in New Orleans had the answer to what had happened and where she'd been. He was reading about the parental kidnapping, and how Millie had finally helped her escape, and as the story continued, learned that she'd been chased down by her own father.

And then he saw the words "five months pregnant… lost the baby…" and froze. His ears were ringing, and the pain in his chest was so severe that he thought he was dying.

"Why didn't I know? Why didn't I know?"

Without hesitation, he picked up his phone and made a call. He didn't know if the number was still good, or if they were even alive, but he had a question only they could answer. The call began to ring, and then an answer. For the first time in eleven years, he was hearing his mother's voice.

"Hello?"

"Mom, it's me!"

Brenda started screaming, "Chuck! Chuck! It's Hunter! He's on the phone." And then he heard his father shouting at him, and realized she put the old landline on speaker.

"Hunt! Where are you? Why haven't you—"

"All those years ago, did you know Lainie was pregnant?"

He heard a gasp, then he heard his mother crying, and his father cursing. He hung up and walked outside.

The lights of Flagstaff lined the horizon to his right. A coyote yipped from somewhere nearby. He looked up. Heaven was littered with stars twinkling within the inky blackness of space. He'd spent more of his adult life in the air than he had on the ground, and always felt lighter and weightless there. But tonight, he'd fallen to earth, and the pain was so great he wasn't sure he could get up. He curled fingers into fists as the stars blurred before him, then the pain came out in a roar, and he kept screaming into the night until the pain bled away.

When he could think without wanting to throw up, he stormed back into the house in long, angry strides, coming out minutes later with his arms full of gear. He threw it all into the back of his Jeep, threw a jacket in the front seat, then went back to lock up and turn out the lights before heading north.

BACK IN NEW ORLEANS, his parents were in an uproar, fighting over who was to blame, and why he'd even asked that question now, after all these years. What happened? What had changed?

It wasn't until they turned on the television for the

local evening news that they got their answer. There was a photo of Lainie Mayes behind the news anchor as he delivered the story.

"One of New Orleans' own has gone missing on a hike in the mountains outside the city of Denver. Twenty-nine-year-old Lainie Mayes, now a resident of Denver, is the object of a massive search. They've been combing the mountains for…"

"Oh, my God. Chuck! Hunt must have seen this report, too. I don't know where he's been, but it's obviously not with her. He's done some digging. But how would he know about…"

"The papers, Brenda. Remember all those ugly stories after her wreck? That shit's on the internet forever now, isn't it?"

"He'll go there, won't he? If she's lost, he'll want to be part of the search," she said. "We need to go now. It may be our only chance to ever see him again."

"I'm not going to drive all the way Denver just to get spit on by my own son," Chuck muttered.

"Fine. I'll go by myself," Brenda said, and left the room.

Chuck followed her to their bedroom. "What are you doing?"

"Packing," she snapped.

He rolled his eyes. "Okay, fine! I'll take you, but I'm telling you now, it's going to be a huge waste of time. We'll leave first thing in the morning."

"If you're going with me, you're leaving tonight," Brenda said.

JUSTIN RANDALL WAS in lockup, still sticking to his story until they gave him reason not to. He sold the same story to his court-appointed lawyer, and wasn't budging. This wasn't his first rodeo, and he'd gotten away with rape accusations before. Granted, none of the other women had gone missing afterward. Whatever happened to Lainie Mayes after she clocked him with that rock was a mystery to him, too. Last time he'd seen her, she was running full tilt down a hiking path.

Chapter Four

Lainie was lost and didn't know it.

It was nearing the end of her second day on the mountain, and she'd stumbled into enough creeks to get water, but her fever was still rising. She had long since lost sight of hiking trails, and while she thought she was traveling long distances, she was actually walking in circles and passing out. She'd forgotten about Justin Randall.

Her focus was on the bear she was convinced was hunting her, and the higher her fever went, the more vivid her hallucinations became. She kept running and hiding, and falling and praying, and when she'd sleep, Hunt was always in the dream.

The bottoms of her socks were beginning to wear. They kept getting caught in rocks and rough ground, and when she sat down, she saw bloody spots seeping through.

Her feet hurt. Her body ached. And the world kept spinning. She'd pass out and wake up on her back, staring up through a maze of green, leafy spires to the clear, cloudless sky above and cry, and then pray.

"Please, God, after all you've taken from me, don't let this place take my life."

GREG AND TINA MAYES reached the Beaver Brook trail-head early, and went straight to the communications station where the searchers were regathering. They'd taken a hiatus after it got dark last night, and this morning, they were going over the maps to the new search grids.

"Excuse me, who's in charge?" Greg asked.

A man in uniform turned around. "That would be me, Scott Christopher. I'm a ranger with the Denver Park Service."

"I'm Greg Mayes, and this is my wife, Tina. We're Lainie's parents, from Baton Rouge. Do you have any news?"

"Beyond finding some of her gear and shoes yesterday, we do not. If you'll give me your contact information and where you're staying, then I can let you know if we have anything new to report."

Greg quickly wrote it all down on a pad the ranger handed him.

"Thank you both. You can wait beyond the roped-off perimeter," he said, and turned his back.

"That was rude," Tina muttered, as they shuffled back to their rental. "Do they expect us to wait out here in the sun all day?"

Greg gave her a look. "We came uninvited. They're searching for our daughter, not asking you to tea. If this is all you can think about, then why the hell did you want to come?"

Tina flushed beneath the sting of his words. Truth hurt. They went back to the SUV in silence, raised the back hatch and crawled inside, then sat down to wait.

Less than an hour later, a dusty black Jeep with Arizona license plates came flying into lot, wheeled into an empty space beyond the perimeter and parked.

"Someone's in a hurry," Greg mumbled.

Tina watched as a tall, dark-haired man unfolded himself from inside the vehicle. He grabbed a hiking pack from the back of the Jeep, then headed toward the communications van at a run.

"Oh, Lord! That's Hunter Gray," Tina said.

Greg frowned. "The hell it is," he muttered, jumped out of the SUV and took off running, with Tina right behind him. Greg cut Hunt off in the middle of the parking lot and put his hand in the middle of his chest. "What the hell do you think you're...?"

Hunt punched him in the face.

Tina gasped, as Greg hit the blacktop on his butt—in shock at the blood spurting from his nose. Then he looked up, past the long legs and broad shoulders into the face of a very angry man with an icy blue glare.

Hunt gave Tina the same look, then toed the bottom of Greg's shoe.

"You don't talk to me. You don't speak my name. Either of you. You don't ever look at me again. I know what you did to Lainie. I know you're responsible for the death of our child. I'm going up that mountain to find her, and alive or dead, I'm not coming back without her. I know you put your hands on her. I know she bled on her bedroom floor. But I didn't know then, what I know now. If she's dead, I will kill you."

It was pure reflex that made Greg flinch as Hunt walked past him, and then he crawled to his feet with blood dripping down the front of his shirt.

Tina was horrified and scurried away, leaving her husband to get himself back to their car. She got her laptop from a tote bag in the front seat, and crawled into the back again. She wanted to know where Hunter Gray had been, and what had happened to turn him into such a savage.

STILL REELING FROM the full-circle moment, Hunt ignored the fact that the perimeter was roped off, and ducked under it before heading to the communications van.

"Who's in charge?" he asked.

"I am," Ranger Christopher said. "Ranger Scott Christopher. And you are?"

"Former Army Warrant Officer Hunter Gray. I spent ten years in the military flying Apache Longbows. Half of that service was spent in Iraqi war zones. I am highly trained in survival and tracking, and I know the woman who's missing. If she's on that mountain, I will find her. May I see the search map? I'd like to know what areas have already been searched, and where you're going today, and your contact number."

Scott blinked. "Uh…do you have some identifications to—"

Hunt whipped out his wallet and started pulling out all kinds of licenses and info, including a wallet-size photo of Lainie's senior year picture, a photo of Hunt and Lainie together, and a photo of Hunt and Preacher on base in Iraq, standing beside their Longbow.

"Miss Mayes's parents are already on-site and—"

"We've spoken," Hunt said. "Now about that map?"

Scott led Hunt inside the communications van, showed

him the map with the grids marked off, then handed him
an unmarked map and gave him a contact number.

"Thank you," Hunt said, entered the number in his
SAT phone contacts, left the van, shifted his backpack
and started up the trailhead.

The sky was clear, and the breeze on the right side of
his face was slight and intermittent as Hunt began the
climb. Now he'd seen the areas that had already been
searched, and the grid they were searching today.

But he was beginning at the spot where her shoes and
gear had been found. That was where she disappeared.
He needed to stand where she'd stood.

He was two miles up the trail before he reached it.
The rangers had marked it with crime scene tape strung
along the area and partway down the slope. He stopped
and looked around, eyeing the trail above, and then
down the slope, trying to imagine her falling. It didn't
compute.

There were no divots in the vegetation, no signs of her
having been grabbing at things trying to gain foothold,
no brush was torn up or broken off. And he already knew
that the backpack had been found in the lower branches
of a tree, not on the ground. So, someone threw it. The
other hiker?

There were tracks all over. Rangers. The searchers.
And God knew who else had walked through here. He
looked farther up the trail and on impulse started jog-
ging. Nearly another mile up, he saw all kinds of debris
in the path before him, and a bloody rock lying off to
the side. Then he saw a torn piece of brown plaid flannel with a white button attached, large boot prints and

smaller sneaker prints. He knelt for a closer look and found three long strands of hair caught in the bark of a broken limb lying on the ground. Auburn hair, like Lainie's.

"You were fighting him, weren't you, baby?" Hunt muttered. "So, is this his blood or yours on this rock?"

When Hunt called down to the communications van, Scott answered.

"Ranger Christopher speaking."

"Scott, this is Hunt Gray. How high have you searched above the place where Lainie's belongings were found?"

"What do you mean, above?" Scott asked.

"Like farther up the trail from where her shoe was found?"

"Well, we haven't, because our initial search began where Justin Randall said they'd been attacked by the bear. But we just got word that the police have Randall in custody. His story isn't checking out. The scratches he has on his face that he claimed were made by the bear were from fingernails."

"I'm close to a mile higher on the trail from where her gear was found. The ground in and around the trail is all torn up. There's debris in the path. I saw three long strands of hair caught in the bark of a branch on the ground. The strands are reddish brown, like hers. There are boot prints and sneaker prints, and a remnant of torn fabric with a button still attached. Looks like from a shirt. There's also a bloody rock on the ground. I think he attacked her here. They fought. She took him out with a rock, disabling him long enough to get away. I don't know if she really did fall, but the tracks I saw while I was going up look like she was coming down at a fast clip."

"Oh, my God. Okay, look, just leave all that as is. I'll get the crime scene crew up there to gather the evidence."

"Will do. I'll continue my searching. If I find anything else, I'll let you know," Hunt said.

"Say, Hunt…what made you think to do that?"

"I don't know. A hunch. Instinct? But I know Lainie. I don't think she fell into that canyon. I'm operating on the fact that she's still alive somewhere until I know different. I'm out."

He put his SAT phone back in his pack, then stood a moment, trying to put himself in Lainie's place and decided to follow the path back down, seeing it from her viewpoint as she was running toward the car park.

When he got back to the point where the first shoe had been found, he stopped, then looked around, then up the trail again, and when he did, this time he realized there was a big dip in the trail. A virtual blind spot.

And then it hit him! What if she knew she couldn't outrun him? What if she faked her own death to escape? But where would she go?

Now his thoughts were spinning, and he was thinking to himself, if she threw her things down the slope, then what? He turned around, looked into the brush and trees on the far side of the trail and started walking.

The ground was littered with pine needles and leaves, and he saw nothing that led him to believe she could have gone this way, but he kept moving, eyes down, looking for footprints, for anything that would tell him she'd been this way.

And then he almost stepped on it. One single foot-print, but not a shoe, like a moccasin, or a sock! A few yards farther, he found another and then realized the prints were going up the mountain now, instead of down, and he remembered something he used to tell her all the time.

When faced with a hard decision, do the unexpected.

"Way to go, baby," Hunt said, and started moving up, following the footprints she was leaving behind. He followed her trail with some ease, and as he approached a large outcrop he could tell from the length of her stride that she was running. And then he saw where she slipped, and the imprint of her body, and blood on a rock, and then the faint imprint of bear tracks, and groaned.

It took a few minutes for him to find the same little footprints leading away from the site. So, she was alive and moving after the fall. The bear tracks were older than her tracks. He needed to believe it was coincidence that they'd crossed, not that she was being followed.

By now, the sun had passed the apex and was moving down toward the treetops. It would be dark in just a few more hours, and he hastened his pace. As long as he could see tracks, he wasn't stopping.

But when he realized he was passing the same dead log a second time, his heart sank. She was walking in circles. Was she hurt and confused from a head injury when she fell? Was she ill? Hallucinating? Or was she just lost and in a panic? He couldn't tell.

Just before dusk, he spotted a large pile of dry brush up against some rocks, studied it for a moment, then walked toward it. That wasn't just random deadfall. The brush had been gathered. After a closer look, he saw handprints in the dirt, and drag marks where she'd crawled beneath a ledge and used the brush as a deterrent against snakes. He admired her foresight, and decided to make a dry camp in the same spot. It was going to be cold, but there was no camping up here. No fires allowed.

He got an LED lantern from his backpack and checked out the area for snakes, then used the deadfall she'd gathered and began pulling it into a circle around him for the same purpose. As he was working, something snapped in the woods behind him. He pulled the 9 mm pistol from his shoulder holster and swept the area with the lantern, suddenly spotlighting a deer in the brush. The animal froze. Hunt immediately turned off the light and heard the deer bounding away in the dark.

He couldn't help but think how helpless Lainie was—injured and alone in the dark, without food, shelter, or any kind of weapon. He wanted to keep searching, but in the dark, it would be a waste of time, so he turned his lantern back on, pulled a blanket from his pack, then some water and jerky. He sat down with his back against the rocks, wrapped the blanket around him, left the lantern on long enough to eat and drink, then turned it off.

He sat in silence while his eyes adjusted to the shadows moving within the moonlight filtering down through the trees, then looked up between the leaves and saw a single, shining star. He hadn't prayed to God in years, but tonight he was asking for a miracle.

"Please, God, I feel her. Just keep her alive until I find her. I'll take it from there."

IT WAS HER on the mountain.

Lainie was curled up in a ball beneath a cluster of deadfalls, created by the hand of Mother Nature, and maybe a little from the hand of God. Over time, branches that had frozen and broken off during past winter storms had formed a kind of shelter for the smaller creatures of the forest.

When she'd first found the spot, she'd crawled into the area on her hands and knees to make a space for herself, and then began breaking off leafy branches from the surrounding underbrush to use for cover over her body before crawling back inside with it.

Now she was lying on her side with the leafy branches over her body, her hands tucked beneath her cheek as the only cushion between her and the cold ground. Her fever was still high, but the cold felt good against her face. She was exhausted, but afraid to close her eyes.

Her body still ached from the brutal attack she'd suffered, but it was her feet that had finally slowed her down. Her frantic need to run had ended. The bottoms of her socks were torn and threadbare; her feet were shredded. The cuts that began healing during the night would only break open every morning when she stood on them, but she'd endured it until she couldn't bear it anymore, and so she'd stopped.

She heard a coyote yip, and another answer, and reached for the chunk of a limb she'd been carrying for a weapon. She didn't have much strength left to swing it, but she had no other options.

The faint scent of skunk drifted past, and then faded. The sound of running water was nearby. She'd walked as far as she could go. The water was close enough to crawl to when she was thirsty, but here she would lie until she was found, or this was where she would die.

She cried a little at the thought. She'd never given up believing they would find each other again, and if she died here, Hunt would be her last thought. She would spend her last breath on his name.

She thought of the ashes of their little baby and cried again. There was an order in her will to be buried with them. The thought of that made her approaching demise less tragic. She'd held the baby in her belly, but she'd never held him in her arms. Dying would remedy that. It would no longer be about leaving this world. It would be about joining her Little Bear in his.

She closed her eyes and drifted off, and suddenly Hunt was before her. When he held out his hand, she took it, and let him lead her into the land of dreams.

It was Hunt's second night on the mountain and he hadn't slept more than an hour or two. He'd already packed up his camp and was just waiting for enough light to track by.

He was eating a protein bar when a porcupine ambled by. His presence startled a gray fox heading back to its burrow for the day. The night birds had gone to roost, and the birds who came with sunrise were already flitting from limb to limb, then dropping to the ground for bugs and grubs. Life abounded, and all he could do was hope Lainie was still part of it.

His wait came to an end in the blink of an eye. The forest went from shadows to daylight, like God walked into the room and turned on a light. He shouldered his pack and started walking in the direction of the last tracks he'd seen—his head down, sweeping the area before him with a clear-eyed intensity. He couldn't afford to miss a clue. Her life depended on it.

LAINIE HAD FALLEN asleep in the night and woke in daylight, burning with fever. Her lips were cracked, and her mouth and throat were so dry she didn't have spit to swallow. She knew enough about the human body that she was severely dehydrated, and if she didn't keep drinking water, her organs would begin shutting down.

She could hear the water in the nearby creek, and getting to it today was her only goal. But when she raised up on her elbow to push the branches aside, the pain that shot up the back of her neck and head was so sharp and sudden that, for a moment, she thought she'd been shot.

"That hurt," she muttered, as she pushed past the pain and started crawling.

But the twenty yards from her shelter to the water might as well have been miles. By the time she got there, her arms were trembling. She went belly down at the water's edge and drank until she could hold no more, and then she ducked her face into the flowing stream over and over, trying to cool the fever, until she finally gave up and crawled the rest of the way into the creek.

The water was barely knee deep, but she floated on

her belly to a partially submerged rock. Using it for an anchor, she wrapped her arms around the projection above the water and held on, letting the cold mountain water be the ice bath she needed.

She was still hanging on to the rock when a possum waddled out of the underbrush and went down to the water to get a drink. The irony of her fighting to stay alive, side by side with a little possum simply quenching its thirst, was a most perfect analogy of life. After it moved back into the underbrush, Lainie began the painful journey of getting herself out of the creek.

By the time she reached the bank and began to crawl up the slope and back to her shelter, she was exhausted. She pulled the branches back around herself, and as she did, realized she'd lost a sock in the creek, then accepted that it no longer mattered. Exhausted beyond words, she rolled over into a ball and closed her eyes. The last thing she remembered was feeling her clothes beginning to dry, and thinking how hungry she was.

GREG AND TINA MAYES were back at the search site again, only this time they'd come prepared. They had folding chairs and a cooler full of drinks and snacks, and were sitting in the shade of a nearby tree.

After they'd gone back to their hotel last night, neither of them had mentioned the obvious, but they both assumed that their daughter was dead. As they sat at the search site this morning, they were actually discussing where Lainie would be laid to rest when an older model Buick drove up.

The moment Greg saw the car, he cursed.

"What in hell makes Chuck Gray think he has business here?" he said.

Tina glanced up and shrugged. "Probably for the same reason we are. Their son. Somehow, they know Hunt's here. You will be civil. They have as much right to be here as we do. You do not get into a shouting match. Do you understand me?"

Greg gave her a look. He knew better than to challenge her with that tone of voice.

"Whatever," Greg said.

CHUCK AND BRENDA GRAY were holding hands as they started across the parking lot when Brenda saw Lainie's parents.

"Greg and Tina are here," she said.

Chuck stopped, stared at them a few moments and then started walking toward them, but it was the women who spoke first.

Brenda nodded at the couple. "Have you been here long?"

"A few days," Tina said.

Brenda hesitated. Her voice was shaky as she spoke. "Do you know if Hunt is here?"

"We saw him," Tina said, then glanced at Greg. His nose was still red and swollen, and he had a fat lip.

"Did he do that?" Chuck asked.

"His version of 'hello,'" Greg snapped.

Brenda ignored him and refocused on Tina. "Did you talk to him? Did he tell you where he's been?"

"He spoke. We listened. It appears he didn't know anything about the past until recently. He is beyond enraged. He's gone up the mountain to look for Lainie. Said he wouldn't be back without her, and if she was dead, he was going to kill Greg when he got back."

Brenda gasped and reached for Chuck's hand. "I told you we should have told him." Tears rolled, and then she wiped them away. "Is there any news about Lainie today? We've heard nothing since we left home."

Tina shrugged. "Not about Lainie, but they arrested the hiker. They think his story was faked. They think she wasn't hiking with him, and that he faked the bear attack to cover up what he'd done to her. They're still searching, but I don't think they believe she's alive."

Brenda was sobbing. "I'm so sorry. We wouldn't be intruding on your space, but we don't know what happened to Hunt." Then she glared at Greg. "He disappeared without a word after his scholarship was rescinded. It's been what…eleven years? We had heard nothing until three nights ago when he called to ask us if we'd known Lainie was pregnant. I didn't know what to say, and I guess our silence was the answer. He hung up, and after we found out about Lainie, I guessed here is where he would come."

Tina glanced at Greg, but he was staring at the ground, so she kept up the conversation. "Hunt doesn't look like he used to. He was a big kid, but now, very much a grown man. And hard…the look in his eyes was frightening. After he went up the mountain, I went online to see if googling his name brought up any answers, but got nothing. Whatever he was involved in, it changed him."

"Probably has a prison record," Greg mumbled.

Chuck's fingers curled into fists. "Well, that's how

stupid you are. That would have been part of public re-cords if you were in a mind to look there. And you're one to talk. He didn't kill his baby. You did that."

Greg started cursing, and Tina dragged him back to where they'd been sitting, while Chuck and Brenda went back to their car. All they could do was sit and wait for Hunt to appear.

PER RANGER CHRISTOPHER'S REQUEST, a crime scene crew from the Denver police had gone up the trail yester-day following Hunt Gray's report. They retrieved hair strands, fabric that matched the flannel shirt they al-ready had in evidence, the bloody rock and took pictures of both sets of footprints. That additional evidence had already been sent to their lab, and if it backed up their suspicions, Justin Randall's story had just blown up in his face.

Ranger Scott had a new search grid for the rescue teams, but hope was fading. It was looking more like they'd be moving from rescue to recovery. He kept hop-ing he'd hear more from Hunter Gray, but after his ini-tial call, the man had gone quiet.

BY NOON, Hunt was finding threads from the socks in her footprints, and sometimes blood on the leaves. He was sick, just thinking of how many times her feet must have been pierced. Her steps were closer together now, and sometimes dragging. He'd quit counting the num-ber of times he'd seen where she fell, and how many times she'd turned around and backtracked after getting up. Following her path was like following a drunk afoot who was trying to find the way home.

And then Hunt crossed a deer trail and lost her. The animals had obliterated all signs of her passing. It was like she disappeared in mid-step. The last time he'd felt this kind of panic was that rainy night in New Orleans, waiting for a phone call that never came.

He did a 360-degree turn, looking for something, anything that would tell him where she'd gone, but there was nothing. He took a deep breath and then shouted. "Lainie! Lainie! Can you hear me?"

He paused, listening. The woods had gone silent. Birds quit calling. Even the breeze had laid.

He shouted again, louder. Longer. "Laàiinnieee!"

Nothing. He started walking in an ever-widening circle for over an hour before he found himself above a creek, and moved down the slope to the water's edge. There were plenty of footprints there, too, but none of them were human.

Heartsick and frustrated, he was about to climb back up when he saw something white caught between the rocks in the middle of the rushing stream. He dropped his backpack on the bank and waded into the water in long, hasty strides all the way to the rocks. Even before he picked it up, he knew what he was looking at. A single white hiking sock, with the sole ripped to shreds. His heart sank as he looked upstream.

"Ah, God…where are you, baby?"

He called her name again, then wrung the water out of the sock and headed back to shore to get his pack.

Now he had a trail again. It was vague, but it was something, and he began walking upstream.

He was still in search mode when he realized the light was beginning to fade. He started running, as if he was trying to outrun the dark, and was about a quarter of mile up the creek when he came full stop, staring at the handprints and crawl marks right in front of him. There were tracks where she'd crawled into the water, and others coming out.

If she was crawling, she couldn't be far!

Shadows were growing longer as he leaped up the creek bank and began following the trail, but he was no longer looking down, he was searching the tree line. She had to be here somewhere.

"Lainie! Lainie! Can you hear me?" he shouted, but the forest had gone silent. He was moving faster now, following the drag marks all the way to a huge pile of dead brush. Stopped by the barrier, he leaned in and then he saw her, curled up on her side, so still and pale he feared the worst.

"Please, God, no," he cried, and began tearing into the brush and limbs, clearing a path to get to her, then dropped to his knees beside her to search for a pulse.

Chapter Five

The pulse was there! A sign of a heartbeat was all he needed. It was a little rapid, but strong and steady beneath his fingers. It was the answer to his prayer. God had kept her alive for him.

"Thank you, Lord. I've got her."

She had the remnants of one sock on her right foot, and her left foot was bare, revealing the wounds. They were red, inflamed, and in a couple of places, oozing pus. But it was the head wound, the horrific bruising from the attack, and the level of fever in her body that frightened him most.

He slipped a hand beneath her neck. She was his Lainie…but different. A woman now, not the girl she'd been. And she was hurt—so hurt.

"Lainie, darlin', it's me, Hunt. Can you hear me?"

She groaned, then sighed as she rolled over and slowly opened her eyes, and stared straight into a piercing blue gaze.

"The raptor found me," she mumbled. "You're here again, Hunt. Are we dead?"

The skin crawled on the back of his neck. Had she been seeing him in her hallucinations?

"No, baby, we're not dead, and I've been looking for you."

She grabbed his hand. "You're really here? My Hunt? You found me?"

"Yes, darlin', I found you. Easy now… I need to see what all has happened to you," he said, and pulled a bottle of water and the first-aid kit out of his pack.

But Lainie wouldn't let him go. She couldn't believe he was real. This was just another awful dream, and he would disappear. In her mind, she needed to keep him talking so he would stay.

"How did you know I was lost?"

"You're all over the news. I heard your name on TV, and I came to find you." He was holding the bottle of water as he lifted her head. "Just a sip, darlin'."

She took a drink and then another one before he set it aside, and pulled out a digital thermometer. The reading came back 104 degrees plus. His heart skipped. That bordered on seizure level. He dug out a bottle of Bactrim tablets, and over-the-counter fever meds, and set them beside his knee.

She couldn't believe he was real and kept staring at him, touching his leg, reaching for his hand, staring into the face of a boy who'd become a man.

"Hunt…all those years ago… I know why you left, but where did you go?"

"To war, Lainie. I went to war."

"In the military? You were in the military?" She shook her head, trying to make sense of what he was saying, still in fear that he was another fever hallucination as he began applying a balm to her lips.

"Army, darlin'. I mustered out months ago. Been flying helicopters for a charter service in Flagstaff ever since," he said, then he reached for the Bactrim and pain and fever meds.

"If I help you sit up, can you swallow these? They're for fever and infection."

She nodded, then shuddered as he moved her to a sitting position.

"Open your mouth, Lainie," he told her, and she did, like a baby bird waiting to be fed. He dropped in the pills, then held a bottle of water to her lips. "Just sip. Don't want to choke you."

She sipped and swallowed, then reached toward his face, running her fingers along a three-day growth of stubble as black as his hair.

"You know how to fly helicopters?"

"I flew Apache Longbows in Iraq for the better part of four years, then off and on elsewhere for the other six."

Her voice shook. "You could have died, and I would never have known it."

He cupped the side of her face. "If it hadn't been for a news report, you could have died, and I would never have known it."

She sighed. "Touché." Then something snapped in the woods behind them, and she went into an all-out panic. "The bear...is it the bear?"

"The bear is gone, baby, and I have a gun. You're safe now. I promise you are safe."

Tears rolled as she began to tremble. "It hurts, and I'm tired, Hunt. I'm so tired of being afraid." Then she touched him again. "Are you real? Is this happening?"

Her confusion was troubling. It could be from the fever, or the head wound, or a combination of both. "I'm as real as it gets," he said, then he took off his jacket and eased her arms into the sleeves. "Here, put this on. You're shaking."

"I crawled in the creek. I thought maybe the cold water would help take down the fever." The weight and the warmth from the jacket was like his hug, as she wrapped herself in it.

He kept thinking of what she'd done to survive, and then realized this wasn't the first time she'd had to run to get away from a monster. He took the bandanna off her forehead and then the other sock off her foot, eyeing the wounds in dismay as he reached into his pack for disinfectant. The last thing he wanted to do was hurt her more, but he had no choice. It was getting dark, and soon be too hard to see. He turned on the LED lantern.

"I need for you to lie down, honey. I'm going to clean up this head wound a little, and I don't want it getting in your eyes."

He made a pillow of his blanket, then eased her down on it.

Her voice was shaking, her eyes welling again with unshed tears. "If I close my eyes, do you promise you won't disappear?"

He leaned down and brushed a kiss across her cheek, then moved the lantern above her head. "I promised you forever. This is me, Lainie. Put your hand on my knee. You'll feel me beside you. You can talk and I'll answer," he said.

He felt her hand on his thigh as he knelt beside her,

then began opening packets of gauze swabs, and dousing them with antiseptic. "Here goes," he said, and began dabbing them along the cut on her forehead. He heard her take a deep breath, then she closed her eyes, but she didn't cry out.

"Did you know the hiker?" he asked, trying to distract her from the pain.

"Stalker from work. Didn't know he'd followed me up the trail. He attacked me, I got away and ran. I tricked him. Made him believe I fell into the canyon, then I did what you always said to do."

He paused and looked up. "What's that?"

"When faced with a difficult situation, do the unexpected. I backtracked on myself and ran up the mountain, instead of trying to get down to the trailhead. When it worked, I thought to myself, Hunter saved me."

Three simple words… *Hunter saved me*, put a lump in his throat. All those years ago, and she'd remembered.

Lainie was still talking. "Then I really did fall later. Hit my head against some rocks. When I woke my head was bleeding, and there were bear tracks all around me. It scared me. I was dizzy and confused and started running. The next morning, I woke up with a fever. I kept getting sicker, then I got lost…so lost, but you kept finding me in the dreams and bringing me back."

Hunt swallowed past the lump in his throat. "Because we belonged. I gave you my heart a long time ago. It will always be yours."

Her hand was still on his thigh when he began making a bandage for her head. "I'm so sorry, Hunt. Sorry I never answered your texts. I didn't see any of them until months later, after I was released from the hospital. Millie took me home to help me pack and get my car, and found my phone under my bed. I guess it fell there when Dad knocked me out."

Hunt frowned, pulled a leaf from out of her hair and then finished wiping down the cut on her head. "I loved you then. I love you now. Nothing will ever change that." He glanced up. It was full on dark now, and he shifted the lantern enough to get a bandage over the cut in her forehead and tape it down. "I'm going to move down to your feet now," he said, and moved the lantern with him.

As he did, he began seeing the rips and tears in her pants and could only imagine how bruised and scratched her legs must be, but he was leaving that to the doctors. Right now, he was most concerned about her feet.

"Lainie, darlin'…you have a lot of open wounds here. I need to clean them out, but you're too hurt. The best I can do is kind of drench them with alcohol. It's going to burn like the devil, but I won't have to touch them."

"It's okay, Hunt. I've outrun the devil before."

In that moment, he felt defeated. He knew what she meant. Despite all of his military service, he had not been a part of their greatest war—the war she'd fought with her family to stay with him. The war that cost them their child.

He opened the bottle, then took a breath. God, he hated doing this. It was going to hurt her even more.

"Are you ready, baby?"

"I'm ready," she said, and held her breath, waiting for the inevitable. But when the alcohol hit the cuts, it felt like she'd walked into fire. She screamed, and then fainted.

The shriek stopped his heart. He was on his knees in seconds, checking for a pulse, but it was steady. He dropped his head, then laid a hand beneath her breasts just to feel her heartbeat.

"I am so sorry, baby. Maybe this way is best. At least you're not going to feel it."

He quickly moved back to where he'd been sitting, put on a pair of surgical gloves and began sluicing alcohol over the bottoms of both feet, pouring slowly, and carefully, making sure he'd gotten it into all of the cuts, then put the lid on the bottle and went back to the first-aid kit for tubes of antibiotic ointment. Working quickly, he liberally applied the contents of the tubes to the bottoms of her feet. Then he stripped off the gloves, dug a clean pair of his own socks from his backpack and slipped them on her feet before rocking back on his heels.

It wasn't nearly all she needed, but it was all that he could do. He was in the act of policing the area for the medical debris he'd discarded, packing it all into a bag to dispose of later, when she woke up screaming his name.

Her panic scared him, and within seconds, he had her in his lap. "I'm here, baby, I'm here."

Lainie opened her eyes, saw his face and went limp.

"Thank God! I thought all of this was another dream. I was afraid to open my eyes and still be alone."

He pulled her closer. "I know we're still sitting in a pile of brush, but you did good finding this place. I'm here and I'm real." He took her hand and put it in the center of his chest. "Feel that heartbeat? That's panic. You passed out from pain and woke up screaming. Damn sure got my attention," he said, then kissed the back of her hand and held it close. "Your feet are all cleaned up, and you're wearing a pair of my socks. Do you feel like you could eat something? I have MREs…meals ready to eat. It's military stuff. Spaghetti, stew, or chili, I think."

"Oh. My Lord. Spaghetti. I choose spaghetti," she said.

"I always knew the way to your heart was to feed you," he said.

"I'd deny that, but it's so the truth."

It was the first time in three days that he'd smiled. "Let's get you settled first," he said, and scooted her out of his lap, and then down between his legs, letting her lean against his chest while he sorted through the food packs. When he found the MRE she wanted, he opened it, handed it to her along with a disposable spoon.

"Lean against me, darlin', and here's your drink. You eat. I'm going to call the ranger in charge of the search parties and let him know I found you, okay?"

"Okay," she said, and then took her first bite of food in three days. It was manna in her mouth.

It was full-on dark, but the lantern shed good light. Good enough for Hunt to see the numbers on the SAT phone. He was relieved by the gusto with which she was eating. She was a raggedy, bloody mess, but she wasn't too sick to eat. He was trying to remember if it was "starve a cold and feed a fever," or the opposite, when the ranger suddenly answered.

"Hello? This is Scott."

"Scott, this is Hunt. I found her. She's alive, mostly cognizant except when she's afraid I'm going to disappear, and wolfing down an MRE as we speak. But she's not out of the woods. She's definitely suffering from dehydration, hypothermia and fever. She wore out her socks walking and running. Her feet are shredded, and infection has set in to some of her wounds. She's running a 104 degree fever, but I just gave her some Bactrim tablets for infection, and some meds for fever. I hope that will offset the worst until we get her down. She's also a lot farther up the mountain from where her belongings were found, but my initial impressions were right. Take my GPS location. She's okay to wait it out until morning, and she's safe here with me now."

"Man…this is the best news ever. I've got a fix on your location. We'll have to pack her back to a trail and then bring her down to where one of the Life Flight choppers can pick her up. You stay put. We'll head your way at daybreak."

"Understood," Hunt said, and disconnected. "Okay, the authorities have been notified, and there will be a lot of happy people tonight. They have been searching hard for you for three days."

She had finished the spaghetti and was licking her spoon when a thought occurred to her. "How did they know I was missing?"

"Not sure why, but the hiker, Randall…took himself to an ER and told some big story about hiking with you and being attacked by a bear."

Lainie tried to laugh, but it came out in a groan. "The

bear was me." And that's when she began to describe the attack in detail.

Hunt could only imagine what Randall must have looked like when he walked into the ER, and kept staring at her. The defiant girl he'd loved had grown into a warrior. But there were pending battles she knew nothing about.

"Your parents were at the trailhead with the search crew when I arrived."

She went pale. "I don't want to see them, ever. Don't let him near me. Please, I—"

"I won't, darlin'. I promise," he said, and then began unrolling the sleeping bag he hadn't used the night before. "It's getting colder, and I need to keep you warm. I'm going to slide in, and then you nestle in against me, and I'll zip us in, then cover us with the blanket, okay?"

Her face was in shadows, but she had an odd expression on her face, and she hadn't answered.

"Lainie...darlin', what's wrong?"

"We've made love a hundred times, but we've never slept together. I never imagined it would happen when I look like and feel like this, or that it would be on a mountain under a pile of brush."

He grinned. "What do we do when faced with a difficult decision?"

She sighed. "The unexpected."

"So...we're right on target," he said. He took the lantern to the sleeping bag, spread it out, then carried her there and laid her down on the outside edge. Then he began pulling all the limbs and brush back into place so they were once again enclosed. He situated his backpack and gun within reach before scooting himself into the bag behind her.

After that, it was a simple matter of zipping them in, spreading the blanket and the sleeping bag over their shoulders before turning off the lantern. Now they were lying on their sides, her back to his chest, with her head beneath his chin, enfolded within his arms.

"My poor, darlin', what a nightmare you have had. Are you okay? Do you need to move to a more comfortable position?"

"I'm okay," she said, but he knew she was crying again.

"I love you, Lainie. Time hasn't changed any of that for me." His voice was a rumble in her ear. She was glad it was dark, and he couldn't see her face, because she had yet to talk about the elephant in the room.

"Hunt…there was a baby."

He took a breath, careful to choose the right words without sounding like an accusation. "I know, honey. I found out after I learned you were missing, but why didn't you tell me?"

His arm was across her shoulders, holding her close. As she reached for him, his fingers curled around her hands.

Her tears were rolling in earnest now.

"I didn't realize it myself until I'd missed my second period, which meant I was nearly two months along. I panicked. I knew what hell the news would unleash, and kept trying to find the right time to tell you, and then I started bleeding, and I thought I'd miscarried."

He hugged her closer, waiting. It was her story to tell.

"But then I didn't have my third period, either, and so I took another pregnancy test, and it was still positive." The timbre of her voice lifted. "I'm not going to lie. I know we didn't plan it, but I was happy. I knew it would be hard, but I figured we'd find a way to make it work once we were both at college. I told myself I could start a year later, and you'd already be there on your scholarship and…well…then it all became moot. Remember when I disappeared the night of the storm?"

He shuddered. "Like it was yesterday. I'd never been so scared."

"That was the day I knew for sure I was still pregnant. I went upstairs to call you, and couldn't find my phone. Then Mother came storming into my room with my phone, screaming at me for being pregnant and ruining all her plans. Dad was worse. They vowed they were going to take me to an abortion clinic the next day. I was screaming at them, telling them if anything happened to me or the baby, I would tell the world what they'd done, and that I would destroy them, and it would ruin their precious social standing." Then she took a deep, shuddering breath. "That's when…that's when…"

Hunt heard the pain in her voice and knew there was something more—something ugly that she couldn't get said.

"What happened, Lainie?"

"Dad flew into a rage. He told me he'd rather the baby and I were dead than have Chuck's child in his family. And then he knocked me out. I woke up in the car. They took me to Baton Rouge to my grandmother's old house and locked me in an upstairs room. I'd been kidnapped, and I was there for two months before I got a chance to escape."

Hunt felt the breath leave his body. There was a roar in his head and a pain in his heart too sharp to bear, and then the sound of his own voice pulled him back.

"Three days ago, I punched Greg Mayes in the face the moment I saw him. I told him if I found you dead, I would kill him. I thought I hated him before, but there are no words for what I'm feeling now. I know he chased you. Did he also cause the wreck?"

Lainie was sobbing now. "Yes. He ran me down and rammed the back of my car trying to make me stop. I lost control. The car went airborne, then rolled and rolled. Our son died, but I didn't. He's a monster and my mother abetted every decision he ever made."

And once again, Hunt was sideswiped. "Son? It was a boy?"

"Yes. I always thought it was a boy, but I didn't know, because they never took me for prenatal care. I asked the doctor after the wreck. He said it was." She paused. Even though she felt the weight of Hunt's body, it was as if he'd turned to stone. He was tense, silent and motionless, and she didn't know how to help him. She'd had all these years to come to terms with what happened, but for Hunt, it was happening now. The only thing she could think to do was make the baby as real for him as he'd been for her. "You know I was alone in my room all the time, except the last month I was there, when they brought Millie down to cook and clean. My mother was such an ass…all pretense of hiding me and my shame, but she still couldn't bring herself to do menial labor. So, I talked to the baby all the time. I called him Little Bear, because every time I got hungry, my stomach would grumble and growl, and I'd chide him for making such noise."

Hunt buried his face at the back of her neck. All the walls he'd put up were crumbling. Four years in Iraq and watching the life leave Preacher's eyes. The suicide bombers. Scrambling to get choppers in the air with sirens blaring. Flying into a hail of ground fire to provide backup for soldiers barricaded in bombed-out villages. Raining Hellfire and Stinger missiles on insurgents while Preacher quoted the Bible from the pilot seat, and people died on the ground. To now, and the shock of learning he'd been a father, and fearing he'd never find Lainie alive. Knowing there'd been a baby, and then hearing her talking about the real baby, the one living within her. The one he'd never known. They'd made a baby, and their fathers' hate for each other had brought his brief little life to an end. He didn't know how to handle all this hate, and at the same time love her this deeply.

His voice was ragged. He had been shattered by what she'd suffered on her own. "I should have been there. I should have found a way. I should have known."

"No, Hunt. He would have killed you. I'm never going to be sorry our baby was here…even if it was just for a little while. I'm sorry you didn't know it then. I'm sorry our parents broke us. But we didn't do anything but love each other. I loved you then. I love you still. Nothing is ever going to change that for me. I'm here now if you still want me."

Hunt groaned. "Want you? Like I want my next breath. I need you to be whole again. I will never make peace with how you've suffered. But I will find peace with you again, and that is enough. Sleep now, darlin'. Tomorrow we get you off this mountain, and we go from there."

Lainie felt lighter. Eleven years of guilt had been a heavy load to carry, and it was gone. "I love you, Hunt."

His voice was a rumble against her ear. "Not a damn ounce more than I love you."

GREG AND TINA MAYES were watching TV in their hotel room when Greg's cell phone rang. When Denver Park Rangers popped up on caller ID, he grabbed it. "Tina, it's the park service!"

"Put it on speaker," she said, and then started weeping. "I'm afraid of what they're going to say."

Greg glared because she was crying again, and then answered.

"This is Greg."

"Mr. Mayes, this is Ranger Christopher from the search site. Hunter Gray just called in. He found Lainie. She's alive, suffering from exposure and some injuries, none of which are life-threatening. He is tending to her immediate needs, and we'll be bringing her down in the morning."

"Thank God," Greg said. "And thanks for letting us know."

"You can thank Warrant Officer Gray and his tracking skills."

Greg frowned. "Warrant officer? What's that?"

"Basically, that's the rank given to Army helicopter

pilots who didn't go through OTS. That's Officer Training School, you know. He spent ten years with the Army before he was mustered out. I know because I checked up on him a little. He flew Apache Longbows in Iraq and Syria in the fight against ISIS."

Greg was so stunned he forgot to respond.

"Mr. Mayes, are you still there?"

"Yes, yes, just taking in what you'd said. Thank you for calling," Greg said, and disconnected.

Tina glared. "So much for your prison theory. Are you going to call Chuck?"

"So he can gloat about his fucking hero son? Hell, no."

She shrugged. "That's okay. I'll call Brenda."

"You don't call her. Do you hear me?" Greg shouted.

"You don't tell me what to do," Tina said. "Not anymore." Then she picked up her phone and locked herself in the adjoining bathroom to make the call.

BRENDA GRAY WAS a mother in mourning. She feared the day Hunt disappeared that he would never be back, and became certain after all the years that had come and gone without a word. She had already accepted he could be dead, and they would never know.

And then he called.

One question. He'd asked them only one question, and her hesitation was their downfall. She could only imagine the shock he'd received, and the hate he must feel. Only after he hung up in her ear did she realize the immensity of damage they'd done. She knew in her heart that seeing him now wouldn't change anything between them, and there was a part of her wishing they hadn't even come.

And then her cell phone rang, and that tiny spark of hope flared as she looked at caller ID. *Tina? Why would she—oh my God... Lainie!*

Chuck hit Mute on the TV remote and looked up. "Who's calling?"

"Tina. It must be about Lainie," she said.

"Put it on speaker. I want to hear," Chuck said.

Brenda nodded, then answered. "Hello?"

"It's me, Tina. I just wanted you to know the ranger called us. Hunt found Lainie alive."

"Oh, my God, Tina! That's wonderful news. I'm so happy for you."

"Well, Lainie won't believe we give a damn about what happens to her, but I'm happy. I just wanted you to know. She has injuries, but none are life-threatening. They said Hunt had administered first aid and was taking care of her. They're bringing her down in the morning."

"Thank you for telling us. We're hoping to get to speak to Hunt then, so we'll see you at the trailhead in the morning."

Tina rolled her eyes. Greg was hammering on the bathroom door and cursing her, but she wasn't finished and went on to tell her what the ranger had told them about Hunt's military service. As she was talking, Greg kicked the door.

TINA ROLLED HER eyes again. "I gotta go. Greg's pitching a fit because I locked myself in the bathroom to call you."

The call ended.

Brenda looked at Chuck. He was smiling.

"That's a son to be proud of," he said.

"If you had been prouder of him before, and less focused on the stupid war with your stepbrother, none of this would have happened," she snapped. "I'm going to bed. We need to be at the trailhead early. I don't want to miss our last chance to see him."

HUNT COULDN'T SLEEP. He'd given Lainie a couple more pain pills in the night. She turned to face him and slid her arm around his upper body as he tucked them back in.

"If this is another dream, I don't want to wake up," she mumbled, and fell back to sleep again with her cheek against his chest.

"Just rest, love," he whispered, and pulled her close.

Night had never been darker. The stars had never been brighter. And the slice of moon was mostly worthless when it came to shining. But it didn't deter the mountain nightlife.

A coyote yipped, and another answered.

Hunt watched a small herd of mule deer move past their shelter, and there was an owl hooting in a nearby tree. Once, he thought he smelled bear, but he didn't hear or see it, and was thankful Lainie was asleep when the odor dissipated.

He kept thinking of all he'd learned, and if anything could be done about it. It enraged him, and it frustrated him that all of it was old news. His only satisfaction was punching Greg Mayes in the face, even before he'd learned the depth of his betrayal.

Then he felt her breathing change. She was dreaming

again. He cupped the back of her head and began whispering in her ear.

"Shush, baby, shush…you're okay. I'm here, I'm here."

She sighed, and then she was still.

THE NIGHT SHIFT was making an exit, and the day shift began arriving. A squirrel was scolding them from a nearby tree, and a little fox passed by them on his way to the creek, and Lainie was awake.

"This is embarrassing, but I need to pee."

He grinned. "Honey, we've seen each other stark naked so many times, I can't believe you'd even utter the word *embarrassing*."

She winced as she tried to move. "Well, it's been a while."

"Better me than the team coming up to get you down the mountain," he said. "Give me a sec."

He tossed their blanket on the pile of deadfall, unzipped the sleeping bag and got up, then began moving aside the limbs to clear their way.

She sat up. "Lord, but I dread walking."

"You're not walking. I'm carrying you into the bushes. As for the rest, I'll close my eyes."

As soon as he had moved enough brush, he grabbed a roll of toilet paper from his pack.

She stared. "What else do you have in there?"

He grinned. "Enough to get by on, and I know what I'm doing, so hush your worries. Today, we blow this Popsicle stand." He handed her the toilet paper, then scooped her up in his arms and headed for the bushes. "Okay, I'm going to ease you down on your feet. I know it's not going to feel good, but those thick socks will help. I'll turn my back, and you let me know when you're done, then I'll go."

He put her down, then held on to her until she'd steadied herself.

"I'm good, and we'll both pee in the bushes. This is my bush. You go find your own."

He was grinning as he walked a couple of yards to comply with her orders, then waited until she called him.

"I'm done."

She was holding the roll of toilet paper when he turned around. It was the first time he'd seen her standing, and he could tell how beautiful her woman body had become. In two strides, she was in his arms again.

"Your Uber has arrived. Where to, lady?"

She smiled. "First pile of brush on your right, please."

He kissed her cheek. "The affection is complimentary. There's no charge for that."

She was still smiling when he put her back down on the sleeping bag, and then reached into the magic backpack again and pulled out a little bottle of liquid hand cleaner. He squirted some in his hands, then handed it to her.

"Wash up, darlin'. Breakfast coming up. We have beef stew with potatoes and vegetables, or chicken and rice with vegetables."

"Chicken and rice, please," she said, as she cleaned her hands.

He glanced at the time, then felt her forehead. It was still too warm, but better than yesterday. He wouldn't rest easy until he had her in the hands of the medics.

But Lainie saw the worry on his face. "It will be okay, Hunt. You already did the hard part. You found me. Once they start pumping me full of antibiotics, then I will be fine."

"You better be," he said, as he opened her food, handed her a spoon and set her drink within reach before choosing beef stew for himself.

Lainie took her first bite, sighing in quiet delight to have food in her belly again. She chewed, swallowed, then licked her spoon.

"You do know that in other circumstances, camping out with you would be a dream. A tent in lieu of dirt. Real food, and a big teddy bear to sleep with. A girl couldn't ask for more."

He was almost smiling. "So, I'm your teddy bear now?"

And just like that, Lainie's teasing ended. "You're my everything. The next time we sleep together, we will make love."

His eyes narrowed, and when she began drawing him a picture, a muscle jerked at the side of his jaw.

She waved her spoon in the air, like a conductor leading an orchestra, illustrating every comment. "I will look and smell pretty then. I will have had a bath and brushed my teeth. My hair will be clean and shiny, and I will wear something sheer and sexy just so you can take it off me."

Hunt's gaze never left her face. "And I will have showered and shaved off this beard, and you must be prepared for me to peel that sexy whatever off of you with my teeth…if it so pleases you."

She shivered. "It pleases me."

"Then it's on my agenda. However, it will please me now if you finish your food, instead of giving me an itch I can't scratch."

"I can do that," she said, and shoveled another spoonful of food into her mouth.

Once they finished eating, Hunt gave her more meds, then settled her on top of the sleeping bag to rest while he went about packing up camp. After that, he sat down beside her and cradled her head in his lap. They talked about nothing, and everything, and he watched her fall asleep in the middle of a sentence and thought he couldn't love her more.

About an hour later, he began hearing voices, and then caught a glimpse of men in the distance, moving toward them through the trees.

"Lainie, honey. They're here."

She rolled over and sat up. "Now what?"

"They'll pack you back to the trail and carry you down to wherever the chopper can land."

"Can you come with me?" she asked.

"Not in the chopper. I'll go back down with the rescue crew after you're loaded, then as soon as I get down the mountain, I'll head straight to whichever hospital they're taking you."

"Surely it will be Denver Health, where I work. If you see my parents down at the trailhead, tell them to go home. I don't want to see them."

"I'll find you wherever you are, and I will send them packing, I promise."

She could see the men now, coming toward them at a jog. "Don't disappear on me."

Hunt stood and then picked her up in his arms. "Don't get lost from me, again."

She wrapped her arms around his neck and started to cry.

"It's okay, love. It's okay," he whispered.

"I know…it's just scary letting go when we just found each other again."

"No more hard decisions to make here. We were always attached at the heart, and nothing has changed. I'll come straight to the hospital. I'll find you there a hell of a lot easier than finding you here."

And then the crew arrived, with Ranger Scott Christopher in the lead. They were elated to see their missing hiker, and praised her for her fortitude, but wasted no time. As they were strapping her down on the stretcher, one of the men handed her a park ranger cap.

"To keep the sun out of your eyes while we're carrying you down," he said. "If it hurts the wound on your forehead, we can adjust the size."

"Thank you," Lainie said. "Much appreciated, and it will be fine." Then she looked around for Hunt.

He was standing just beyond the stretcher with the magic backpack on his shoulder, his gaze focused on her, and everything they were doing.

"I'm here," he said. "The path will be narrow, so even if you can't see me, remember I've got your back."

Then they picked her up and started walking.

Hunt gave the giant brush pile one last glance, thankful it had been a shelter and not a grave, then fell into step.

BOTH SETS OF parents were on the scene, but sitting on opposite sides of the parking lot.

Greg and Tina were still fussing.

Chuck and Brenda were silent.

None of them knew Lainie was being airlifted, or that it would be Hunt who reached the trailhead alone. They kept glancing at each other and then looking away. They'd come to this place because of guilt and duty, but everything about this day felt wrong. They'd gate-crashed a reunion to which they no longer belonged.

IT HAD TAKEN the recovery team a little over an hour to hike out of the woods and back onto the trail. They'd been walking it for a while when Hunt began hearing the familiar blade slap of rotors. His pulse quickened, and then he heard Scott talking to Lainie.

"The chopper's inbound. We're almost there, Miss Mayes. Are you okay?"

"I'm okay. Where's Hunt?"

He glanced over his shoulder. "Behind us. He took the flank position, but you will see him before you leave. He'll help load you up."

Her throat tightened with yet another overwhelming urge to cry, but she wouldn't. She didn't want his last sight of her here to be in tears.

A small clearing on the south side of the trail became visible as they came out of the trees. A Classic Air medical copter was already down, rotors still spinning, with the doors open, waiting to hot load. The recovery crew immediately left the trail with Lainie and headed toward it.

Hunt dropped his pack on the trail and ran to catch up. She reached for his hand the moment she saw him, and then he ran the rest of the way with her. One quick kiss, and then he helped lift her up into the chopper. He got one last look at her face before the doors shut between them, and then he was running to get away from the downdraft as it lifted off.

Scott and the recovery crew were already heading down the trail when he grabbed his backpack and caught up.

"Where are they taking her?" he asked.

"Where she works—Denver Health Hospital," Scott said. "They will be waiting for her."

"I'll find it. A big thanks to all of you, but here's where we part company," he said, and started down the trail at a lope.

"Damn, does he think he's going to run the whole way down?" one man asked.

"He's Army, man. He can probably run circles around us and then some," Scott said. "Besides, I think he's got a woman to see about the rest of his life."

Chapter Six

Lainie felt the chopper lift off, and then an EMT began taking vitals, while the nurse on board started an IV. They were talking to each other on their headsets, but the noise inside the chopper made hearing them impossible, so she laid still and closed her eyes. The end of this journey was where her healing began.

The trip was brief. The landing, little more than a bump, and they were down. The doors opened then they were pulling her out on the gurney and pushing her toward the hospital on the run.

The spinning rotors whipped the air into a frenzy, while the heat coming off the roof washed over her in a wave. She closed her eyes against the glare, and only knew they were inside the building by the sudden waft of cool air and people saying her name. Then they were on the move again, pushing her to the dedicated elevator that would take her down to ER.

IT WAS CHARIS's day off, but she'd heard the new update early this morning that Lainie had been found alive, and the rescuers would be bringing her down the mountain today.

Charis had cried buckets when Lainie went missing, and now, knowing she had been found by the man she'd loved and lost, was like something out of a fairy tale. She was guessing they were using a chopper to pick her up somewhere along the trail, but without knowing the schedule or the ETA, she just went straight to the emergency room to wait for her arrival.

A couple of hours passed before they got word the chopper had landed. At that point, the ER erupted in a scurry of doctors and nurses readying for her arrival, along with a detective from the Denver PD, and a crime scene investigator.

Suddenly the paramedics appeared with their patient and rolled her into an exam room then transferred her to the bed as they were debriefing the waiting staff on her stats and condition.

Between the pain and fever, the trip down the mountain and then the chopper noise, Lainie arrived in the ER with a pounding headache and was on the verge of nausea. The room was spinning, and she was afraid she'd pass out when she suddenly spotted Charis at the door.

"Charis. I need to talk to Charis."

Charis hurried into the room. "I'm here, honey… I'm here."

"Hunt will be coming. Can you watch for him, and tell him what's happening and where I am so he doesn't tear up the hospital looking for me?"

"Of course, but how will I know him?" Charis asked.

"Look for tall, dark and handsome, ice-blue eyes, devil-black hair and stubble to match, and if you hear Louisiana coming out of his mouth, that's him."

"Consider it done," Charis said, and left on the run, while one of the other nurses looked at Lainie and groaned. "Dang, girl. Does he have a brother?"

"No, and hands off," she mumbled.

All of the staff in the room knew Lainie, which made what was happening personal to everyone, including her, but when they began cutting off her clothes, she had no recourse but to let it happen.

Clay Wagner, the ER doctor, quickly moved to the side of her bed. "Welcome back, Lainie, and apologies upfront before we start. This is Della Pryor, a detective with the Denver PD, and she's brought a tech from the crime lab with her. They'll be taking photos of your injuries to back up their case against Justin Randall."

Lainie winced as they kept cutting off her clothes. "Whatever it takes to put him away. And don't lose the car keys in my pocket!"

Wagner continued his examination as every garment was cut away, and when more injuries were revealed, photos were quickly taken. They had her down to socks and panties when Detective Pryor asked them to turn Lainie on her side long enough for them to get photos of her back.

The scrapes and bruises visible there were purple, telltale evidence of the fingerprint bruises on her shoulders and neck where Justin Randall tried to hold her down. Being manhandled exacerbated the pain, but Lainie said nothing, and then they took off her socks.

There was a mutual gasp at the sight and then she heard someone crying. It wasn't as if they hadn't seen worse. It was just because they knew her, and knew everything she'd endured to stay alive. Lainie felt tears welling, and blurted out a joke to change the emotionally charged moment.

"Come on, guys, they feel even worse than they look, so nobody gets to cry but me."

Joking among themselves was how doctors and nurses got through the trauma of what they saw, and the ensuing laughter shifted their emotions.

"Do we need to do a rape kit?" Pryor asked.

Lainie shook her head. "No, ma'am. He only wished. All we had was a nasty wrestling match, and I took him out with a rock before he could unzip his own pants."

"Noted," Pryor said. "We do need to collect DNA from beneath your fingernails. It won't take long." She then signaled her tech, who quickly gloved up and began taking scrapings from under Lainie's nails.

"Apologies for invading the ER and your personal space, but I think we're done here," Pryor said, and she and the tech left the room.

The staff covered Lainie with a sheet, as a tech rolled in a portable X-ray, followed by a lab tech who'd come to draw blood.

Dr. Wagner moved to the foot of the bed to check her feet and the depth of the cuts, but at the first sign of pressure, Lainie screamed.

Wagner jumped. "I'm so sorry. I didn't realize… As I look at the damage here, I think I'll be better able to treat you if we do this in surgery, so we're going to put you under."

Still reeling from the pain, Lainie's voice was shaking, but it was the best thing she'd heard since her arrival. "I second your suggestion, but you might want to run me through the car wash before you start."

They laughed again.

"Having spent four days lost on a mountain, you don't look so bad," Wagner said.

"It was probably the soaking I took from that last creek I crawled into trying to bring down my fever. You know what they say in Texas about women's big hairdos? The higher the hair, the closer to God? I can testify in all honesty that God did not pipe in hot water up there."

They were still laughing when they wheeled her out of the room.

BY THE TIME Hunt reached the trailhead, he was exhausted. His clothes were drenched with sweat, and he was in no mood for the reunion he knew was waiting. What he didn't expect were his parents on the scene, as well, but there they were, all running toward him with panicked expressions on their faces. His first thought was, *What the hell?* then he tuned in to what they were saying.

"Where's Lainie? What happened?" Tina screamed.

Hunt dropped his backpack, started to reach into an outside pocket for something to wipe off the sweat, then used his shirtsleeve, instead.

"Nothing happened. A med-flight chopper picked her up halfway down."

"What hospital? Where?" Greg shouted.

The moment Hunt heard that voice, he turned to face him, his voice deepening in anger with every word that he spoke.

"I told you, never look at me again. Never talk to me. Never speak my name." Then he stared Tina down until she took a step back. "Lainie sent you two a message. She doesn't want to see you. She doesn't want to hear your voices, or see your faces. Ever. You don't go to the hospital. You don't interfere in any part of her existence, ever again. You lost the right to her the day she was knocked unconscious in her own bedroom. You kidnapped her like a criminal and locked her up in a velvet jail."

Hunt's rage was frightening, and Greg made a crawdad move backward as Hunt moved toward him, so close now that Hunt could see blood pulsing through a bulging vein in the old man's forehead.

"I don't know who you paid off to get away with what you did, but I know the truth. You ran your daughter down, rammed the back end of her car and caused the wreck."

Greg's face was flushed. His eyes were bulging with a level of fear and anger that he didn't dare turn loose, then when Hunt took another step toward him, it was all he could do not to turn and run.

"You killed my son. And you tried to kill Lainie because of your bullshit feud with my father. The only reason you're still breathing is because she's still alive. Now get in your car and get the hell out of my sight. Both of you!"

The rage in his voice sliced through them. Tina slid her hand under Greg's elbow as Hunt turned to his parents.

"I don't even know what to say to you, but I don't know you anymore. You betrayed me in a way that should haunt you for the rest of your lives. Your silence abetted Lainie's abduction. Your continuing silence led to the death of your own grandchild. You all fed off a war that had nothing to do with the children you both bore. You gave us life, and then you broke us. Lainie and I were pawns. You tossed us about like grenades, daring each other to pull the pins. And when you finally did, we became collateral damage."

Chuck was pale and Brenda was weeping.

"I'm sorry, son," Chuck said.

"No, you're not, and don't call me 'son.'"

Hunt shuddered. He felt empty. Like all the negativity they'd fed him was gone. They were staring at him, pale-faced and silent. His parents. Her parents. All of them. For the first time holding and owning their guilt.

"I don't know how your lives are going to end, but I know Lainie and I will thrive without you. You men are worthless. Whatever tiny bits of good you have put out into this world, you have negated it a thousand times over with your hate. When you die, they should burn you into ashes, bury you both in the same unmarked hole, then forget you ever existed. You have wasted your entire lives fighting over nothing but a common dislike for each other, so you should spend eternity together. And if God wants your sorry souls back, He'll know where to find them."

Greg shuddered, and Chuck was slack-jawed in disbelief. Had Hunt just heaped a curse upon their souls? They wouldn't look at their wives, and they wouldn't look at each other. But they were all watching Hunt as he picked up his backpack and walked away, and they were still watching when tossed his backpack inside his Jeep and began stripping down to his briefs.

Even from a distance, they could see the man and muscle the Army had built, and to their horror, the scars it had left behind. They were still watching when he retrieved clean clothes from the back seat, then put them on and drove away.

The parents parted company without a word. It was going to be a long silent drive back to Louisiana for all of them, with plenty of time to reflect on what they'd wrought.

As they were driving away, Hunt was entering the hospital address into his GPS. He followed them all the way to Denver Health, eyeing the massive edifice as he pulled into the parking lot, then drove to the emergency room entrance and parked. He grabbed his backpack as he was getting out, and hurried inside.

CHARIS HAD BEEN in the ER lobby for hours, eyeballing every man who walked in. She knew it would take time for Hunter Gray to get off the mountain and then back into the city, but it didn't matter. She was here for Lainie.

And then she saw a man coming toward the entrance. His head was up, and he was moving at a fast pace, with a trail-dusty backpack slung over one shoulder.

The moment he entered the lobby, she knew it was him. Tall, dark and handsome didn't cover it, and even though she was close to the date of her own wedding, just looking at him sent shivers up her spine. She jumped up, running.

"Excuse me! Excuse me! Are you Hunter Gray?"

Hunt skidded to a stop and turned around. "Yes. Who are you?"

Charis sighed. "The scout your girl sent to find you."

His relief was evident. "She's okay?"

"Yes, or will be. They took her to surgery to—"

He panicked. What had he missed? Did delaying her retrieval make it worse?

"Why surgery? What happened?"

"I'm sorry. Nothing dire. They decided anesthesia was the best option before they began treating her feet."

"Oh, right," he said. "She passed out last night when I started pouring disinfectant on them. It scared the hell out of me. Can you tell me where she is?"

"Consider me your escort. I work here, too, although this is my day off. I'm to take you to her room."

"Yes, ma'am. Lead the way."

"Oh, by the way. My name is Charis, and Lainie is one of my best friends."

BETWEEN THE DRUGS, the shampoo, and the bed bath they'd given her, Lainie was feeling no pain—or at least, not much. But being a patient here was the flip side of her daily life. In here, she felt isolated from everything.

She frowned as she fingered her scalp around the head wound. They'd shaved a little bit of hair away to staple it up, so she'd chosen not to look at herself in a mirror. The expressions of horror on her friends' faces when they'd first seen her said it all.

She quit fiddling with the staples, and was staring at the ceiling and thinking about Hunt when someone knocked, and then the door swung inward.

Charis came through, then stepped aside. "Mission accomplished, dear friend. Rest well. We'll talk another time," she said, then blew her a kiss and left the room as the door swung shut behind Hunt.

Seconds later, he was at her bedside. He dropped his backpack to embrace her, then froze. Between the stitches in her head, the bandages on her feet and the cuts still healing on her lips, he was afraid to touch her body at all, and took her hand instead.

"Hey, baby…what did they say? What all did they do? Are you hurting?"

"Pain-wise, I'm better now. I have a concussion, which is healing in spite of me. Bruised ribs but nothing broken. The obvious staples in my head. I'm told that after they cleaned my feet, they glued the deep cuts, and left the rest to heal on their own. A couple of places were infected, as you know, but I have double doses of antibiotics in me, and enough pain meds in me to make the world look pretty in pink."

He smiled. "I'd almost forgotten your sense of humor, and now I'm wondering what kind of description you gave to your friend that made her identify me so fast."

"Oh…basically just look for the best-looking guy with black stubble," she said, and ran her fingers against his chin.

"Ah, yes… I'm going to have to deal with all that."

"They're going to let me go home tomorrow. I'm still here only because they administered anesthetic. When do you have to go back to work?"

His eyes darkened. "Never. I'm not leaving you."

"But your job?"

"Darlin', I can fly choppers anywhere. However, I may be ahead of myself. I guess I need to ask, is there still room for me in your world?"

"Dumbest question ever, and yes," she said. "I have a house. I bought it years ago. I love the house. Everything I did to it was with you in my heart. I guess I should have sent out an SOS years ago, but I think I was afraid to face you."

"Well, that's bullshit, and now you know it," Hunt said. "Then it's settled. I'll call my boss, Pete, and tell him I'm staying. I can catch a quick flight back in a few days to pack up my clothes, and we'll go from there."

Tears quickened. "Go from there… We finally have a future, don't we?"

"Yes, ma'am, we do, but we can't go back. Life happened. We both changed, but without each other to monitor the changes. We're gonna take this slow and this time, do it right. No running. No hiding. We already love each other. We just need to feel the solid ground beneath our feet here as well," he said, and brushed a kiss across her forehead.

She was crying again. "Thank you for coming to find me. Thank you for still loving me even after all the chaos my parents caused. I'm so sorry about your scholarship. I cannot imagine how that felt."

Hunt slid his hand beneath her palm and felt her fingers curl around it. Just like they were before—always needing that feeling of connection. She'd bared her soul to him on the mountain, and he was still living with his hell. It wasn't fair to her, and there were things he needed to purge. They were already talking about their future, and he was still buried in the past.

"I need to tell you stuff, but at the same time, I keep thinking, wait until she's better. Only we both learned the hard way what happens when you wait."

Lainie tightened her grip on his hand. "Lower this bed rail and sit down beside me. Whatever it is will never change how I love you. Give *me* your demons to hold. I know how to handle them."

Hunt lowered the railing, then scooted onto the side of the bed. He glanced at her once, then dropped his head.

Lainie reached for his hand as she waited. She could feel the tension in his body and gave his hand a little tug. "Hunter, it's okay."

He took a deep breath and started talking.

"I've never talked about this before, and you deserve to know. Because there can't be secrets between us again. Ever. I have nightmares that will never go away. Just as I'm sure you do. But you told me yours. And I need to tell you mine."

"I'm listening," Lainie said.

Hunt nodded. "I shut down after I left New Orleans. I packed up the boy I'd been and tried to forget he'd ever existed. There were days in Iraq when I thought I would probably die. Looking back, I think I joined the Army expecting it to happen. By a twist of fate and an aptitude test, I wound up in Aviation training and came out good at what I had learned to do. The whole time I was deployed, I carried out my job in the cockpit of an Apache Longbow, the Army's most impenetrable helicopter. I occupied the front seat as gunner and copilot, with my pilot, Preacher, behind me quoting Bible verses as he flew. Every pilot has a call sign. They called me Gator because I was from Louisiana. There were days when we felt invincible, and days it felt like not even God could save us. Yes, we got shot at every time we went up. And yes, they threw everything at us from ground fire to blasting at us with RPGs, and MANPADS. But we were in Longbows, and what we didn't evade was deflected. We were not on the ground like foot soldiers, being moved from place to place in truck convoys, riding along with your buddies in the middle of nowhere and getting blown up by an IED while you're in the middle of laughing at someone else's dirty joke. But pilots did die. And war sucks. You know?"

Lainie's heart was hammering. She could feel every nuance of the nightmares within him, and yet there were no platitudes that fit. No words to take away the pain, so she did what he needed most, and just listened and watched the shadows come and go on his face.

He was staring out a window now as he talked. She knew he'd gone back there in his mind, and there was no way for her to follow.

He glanced back at her face. She hadn't flinched, and this was good, because it was her permission he sought, to be able to continue.

"We'd been in-country for almost eighteen months and were having a little downtime at the base. It was hot and sunny, and the endless wind was blowing sand in our hair and in our eyes, and if we laughed, we had grit in our mouths, but on that day it didn't matter. We were just hanging out, playing a game of pickup. Rat had the basketball. I was defending under the basket. T-Bone was dancing around in the corner, waving his hand for a pass, and Preacher was coming in behind Rat for a steal when a sniper hiding in the surrounding mountains fired a shot. Preacher had this look of surprise on his face." Hunt stopped, swallowing past the lump in his throat. "And then I saw the hole in his forehead about a second before the next shot hit me in the back."

Lainie flinched. He'd never said he'd been shot!

Hunt looked up and out the window again. "I watched him die in front of me. The last thing I saw before I passed out was Rat running for a weapon. Preacher died and I didn't, and guilt set in. I didn't want to get close to anyone like that again. I'd lost you and then him, so I shut down emotionally and focused on nothing but what I'd signed up to do. Even after we were stateside again, and then deployed in different places during the ensuing years, I began to burn out. Ultimately, I left because I was tired of running away from the past. Then I saw your story on the evening news, and the rest you know."

TEARS WERE RUNNING down her face. "Oh, Hunt… I need to hug the hurt out of you so bad I can't stand it, and they've hooked me up to everything in this hospital except WiFi. Come lie down beside me. You've stayed awake for days because of me. Let *me* hold *you* now while you sleep."

He damn sure wasn't leaving her and didn't have it in him to refuse that offer. And, since she hadn't thrown up her hands in shock at what he'd told her, he guessed she'd decided to keep him.

"You know it's against the rules?"

"You leave the demons and the rules to me," she said, and scooted over until her back was against the bed rail.

Hunt kicked off his boots, lay down beside her and pulled up the bed rail, then turned to face her with the railing at his back. He searched her face for doubt and saw none. All he felt was love. He'd bared his soul, and now his heart was in her hands.

"I love you, Lainie."

She sighed. "I love you, more."

"We're breaking all kinds of hospital protocol," he said.

"I am a dear and beloved employee here, and you're already everybody's hero because you found me, so, in their eyes, you can do no wrong. I love you. Close your eyes."

So, he did.

Chapter Seven

It was time for evening meds.

Lainie's assigned nurse, Maggie Rae, was making her rounds when she entered Lainie's room, then came to a full stop. There was a grown-ass man in bed with her patient, sound asleep and stretched out beside her with his feet hanging off the side. Then she realized it must be Hunter Gray, the man who'd found her.

Gossip was they'd known each other before, and it must have been something special for him to come from so far away to search. Even now, he'd put himself between Lainie and the door, with his arm across her waist in a gesture of protection.

Lainie heard footsteps approaching her bed and opened her eyes, then put a finger to her lips and whispered, "He never slept until he found me."

Maggie lowered her voice as she began checking Lainie's stats. "Bless him. He's quite the hero. How are you feeling?"

Lainie sighed. "Everything hurts."

"This should help," Maggie said as she injected the syringe full of pain meds into Lainie's IV port. "There you go, honey. You'll get easy soon. Do you need anything?"

Lainie looked down at the man beside her. "Not anymore." Then closed her eyes.

JUSTIN RANDALL HAD been taken in handcuffs from his jail cell to an interrogation room. The guards seated him at a table, then one stayed on guard with him. All Justin knew was that his lawyer was coming, so he settled in to wait, but not for long.

Minutes later, the door opened, and Richard Stovall, his court-appointed lawyer, entered the room.

"I'll need some time alone with my client," Richard said.

The guard left the room as Richard sat down and flipped open a file.

"I'll get right to it. You have problems," Richard said. "Lainie Mayes was found alive this morning. She has a large number of injuries, some of which back up the police's theory that you attacked her, and she had plenty to say about that. The lab reports came back regarding DNA found on evidence from the scene of the attack, as well as DNA taken from her backpack they found in the canyon. It's yours."

"Okay, so there wasn't any bear attack, but I didn't try to kill her," Justin said. "She got herself lost."

"Running away in fear for her life after you assaulted her," Richard said. "I'm told the cops were at the emergency room when they brought her in. They took scraping from beneath her fingernails to test for DNA." Then he looked straight at the scratches on his client's face. "We both know how that's going to turn out. And that's not all. About twenty-four hours after your name was mentioned as a suspect of interest in the local and national news, four other women have come forward, claiming you both raped and assaulted them, and threatened to kill them if they talked."

Justin blinked. "They can't prove any of that. It will be my word against theirs."

"So, it's true?" Richard asked.

"Can I fight this?" Justin asked.

"You have no grounds to fight with," Richard said. "Whatever happens, you're going to prison. It's the sentencing that will determine the time you will serve."

Justin shrugged. "Win some. Lose some."

SOMEONE LAUGHED IN the hall outside Lainie's room.

The sound woke Hunt abruptly from a dreamless sleep, and the first thing he saw was her face. She was sound asleep with lashes fluttering, and a tear on her cheek. She was dreaming. *This is real. This is happening.* Bruised and battered, and she'd never been more beautiful to him. *Thank you, God.*

He eased over onto his back to lower the bed rail and stood up, then slid his hands beneath Lainie and slowly eased her back to the middle of the bed. She moaned, then sighed as Hunt pulled the covers up over her shoulders, brushed a kiss across her cheek, then pulled up the bed rail and headed for her bathroom with his backpack.

LAINIE HAD A brief moment of fright when she woke up alone, then she heard water running in the adjoining bathroom and relaxed. Hunt was in the shower. All was right with her world.

She listened, taking comfort in the sound of his presence until the water stopped, then she heard him moving around and thought of all the mornings of their life ahead. Going to bed together. Waking up the same way. And the sound of a shower. She'd never had the pleasure of his company in this way, and was anticipating the simple acts of life that came with love.

And then he emerged, dressed all but for the clean T-shirt he was holding, and she forgot to breathe. The stubble was gone, and the man he'd become was standing before her. Zero body fat. Chiseled abs. A jawline to die for. Blue eyes flashing. The same sensual mouth and thick black hair. And the remnants of war on his body and in his gaze.

She sighed. "So. You have grown into a magnificent man."

The corner of his mouth tilted, just enough to pass for a smile as he approached the bed. "I guess we can chalk it up to Uncle Sam's good cooking," he drawled.

"Nope. I knew you when, remember? This was always you, just waiting to turn into this."

"If you say so," he said, and smoothed the flyaway strands of hair from her face.

"Show me," she said.

He frowned. "Show you what?"

"Where the bullet went in your back."

He turned, then raised his arm a little. "It went in there and came out here." Then he pulled the T-shirt over his head and ended the search as he glanced out the window. The sky was changing. Evening, and they were no longer on the mountain.

The door opened behind him, bringing the scents of food with it. Meal carts were in the hall, and nurses came into her room with two trays. One for Lainie. One for Hunt.

"Maggie Rae ordered two trays for this room," the nurse said.

Hunt glanced back at Lainie. "Who's Maggie Rae?"

"The nurse who caught you sleeping in my bed."

He grinned. "So, I'm not going to be shot at sunrise, after all?"

"I told you I had friends here," Lainie said.

They put Lainie's tray on her tray table and the second one on the window ledge for Hunt.

He lifted the food covers. "Thank you, ladies. This looks and smells way better than the MREs we were eating, doesn't it, darlin'?"

Lainie frowned. "I don't know about that. That first packet of spaghetti with meat sauce tasted like heaven after three days with nothing but water." Then she gave Hunt a look. "Or maybe it was just the chef that made it so good."

"Yeah… I fed you, then poured alcohol on your feet and made you faint. I'll never get over that," he muttered.

The nurses left, and as soon as Lainie raised the head of her bed and moved her tray table toward her, he pulled up the big recliner and sat down beside her with his tray.

"I don't always pack MREs," he said. "When I have to, I'm a fair cook."

"No worries, sweetheart. I love to cook, and I'm better than good." Then she took her first bite. "Um, almost Salisbury steak."

Hunt grinned. "So, a hamburger patty in sauce?"

She nodded and took another bite, and so it went. They were down to scraping the bottom of their pudding cups when Dr. Wagner came in with his nurse, making rounds.

"Good evening, Lainie. Who's your dinner partner?" he asked.

"Hunter Gray. Childhood sweetheart. Man of my dreams. Also, the man who found me. Hunt, this is Dr. Wagner. The man with the staple gun and anesthesia."

Wagner grinned. The hospital staff was well aware of Lainie Mayes's wicked sense of humor.

Hunt immediately stood and shook the doctor's hand. "It's a pleasure, sir."

Wagner arched an eyebrow. "That was very military. Did you serve?"

Hunt nodded. "Ten years. I'm out now. Been flying charters for Randolph Charter Service in Flagstaff, but I'll be staying here in Denver."

"Good. That means you're not sweeping Lainie away from us. She is a very valuable employee, as well as a good friend. We'd hate to lose her." Then Wagner switched focus and moved closer to Lainie's bed. "The wound in your head looks good. Shirley is going to unwrap your feet for me. I need to make sure everything looks okay before I let you go home tomorrow."

Hunt moved out of the way, but stayed close enough to get a good view after the bandages were removed.

"The antibiotics are already working," Wagner said.

"The infected areas are looking much better, and the more superficial cuts are already starting to seal up."

"How long will it be before I can walk?" Lainie asked.

"Don't rush it, but I'd say, as soon as you can comfortably bear weight. You'll need to be cleared before you come back to work, but take the time to heal without worry. Your job isn't going anywhere."

"What happened to the clothes I was wearing when they brought me in?" she asked.

"We cut them off, remember?" Wagner said.

"I had a set of car keys in my pocket. I'm going to need them. And now that I think of it, my car is still parked at the trailhead."

"I believe your keys were bagged and tagged and are at the nurses' desk. Shirley will check for you when we're done here," he said.

"Will I need to change bandages daily?" Lainie asked.

"Maybe for another day or so. After that, I think heavy socks should suffice. Definitely no shoes until you can walk comfortably, and then something like a slipper."

"She's got me," Hunt said. "I waited eleven years to find her. I've got no problem carrying her."

Wagner nodded.

Lainie teared. She made jokes to hide her fears, while Hunt simply blurted out his truths. When the nurse began putting fresh bandages on Lainie's feet, Hunt reached for her hand. She clung to him without words, and soon they had the room to themselves again.

"Don't worry about your car. Once we get you home and I get you settled, I can take an Uber back to the park to get it," Hunt said.

Tears rolled.

Hunt groaned, and then lowered a bed rail and slid onto the bed beside Lainie. He slipped his arms around her. "Honey…what's wrong?"

"Nothing. Just a little PTSD, and not used to having anyone help me do anything."

"Understood," he said. "Tomorrow is the beginning of us again. You and me. For the first time in our lives, we'll be together and on our own."

As PROMISED, Lainie was released the next morning after Wagner made rounds. Hunt had already filled her prescriptions at the hospital pharmacy, and was waiting outside the hospital entrance with the passenger door open. Lainie was wearing borrowed scrubs and another pair of his socks when the orderly brought her down in a wheelchair. It was gray and cloudy, with a forecast of thunderstorms, and Hunt wanted to get her home before they hit.

"Did they give you your keys?" he asked as he picked her up and settled her into the front seat.

"Yes, right here," she said, and held up a plastic bag with her release papers and the keys safely inside.

He buckled her in, then kissed the side of her cheek. "Love you," he whispered, then stepped back and closed the door as the orderly took the wheelchair back inside.

Moments later, he was behind the wheel. He reached across the console and gave her hand a quick squeeze, then reached for his phone.

"I need an address now, darlin', because I don't know where you live."

Lainie blinked. "Oh, right! I guess you do."

He entered it into his GPS and then drove away, following the route, while the clouds continued to gather and the sky began to darken. Twenty minutes later, he pulled into her driveway.

"I'm going to guess the remote control to your garage is in your car," he said.

"Yes, but there's a keyless entry pad on the outside. The four number code is your birthday—1010. Just key it in."

He smiled, gave her a thumbs-up and got out running. The wind was rising, and the first drops of rain were already falling as he keyed in the numbers. When the door began to go up, he ran back to the Jeep and drove into the garage.

"Just in time," Hunt said.

She sighed. "Home. There was a time when I didn't think I would make it back here."

"Will the door into the house be locked from here?"

She shook her head.

"Then sit tight. I've always dreamed of carrying you across the threshold, just not exactly like this."

Lainie was still smiling when he lifted her from the front seat and headed for the door. She hit the Down button on the keypad to lower the garage door as they went by, and then they were going through a utility room and into the kitchen/dining area.

Hunt paused, admiring the open concept of the house.

"This is incredible. It feels like you. Where do you want to be, darlin'? Your bedroom, or on the living room sofa for a bit?"

"The sofa."

Outside, the sprinkles were turning into a torrential downpour as Hunt carried her toward a blue upholstered sectional.

She looked toward the window and shivered. "Thank God I am not still lost on that mountain."

"I don't want to think about it," he muttered as he put her down. "I'm going to get my gear. I'll be right back," he said, and bolted back toward the garage.

When he came back carrying it, she waved him down the hall. "My bedroom is the big one at the end of the hall. You'll have to give yourself the grand tour."

He made quick work of the trip, eyed the king-size, four-poster bed, then dumped his stuff just inside the door and returned to where she was sitting.

"Do you need anything, honey? Bathroom? Something to eat or drink?"

She glanced at her little brown teddy with the wobbly head. "Not now, love. Come sit with me for a bit."

Hunt was wondering how he would fit into this place of calm and peace. This was her space. He'd played no part in her life here, but he had no words for how grateful he was to be here.

He was moving toward the sofa when a little wooden rocker at the corner of the hearth caught his eye, and then he recognized the teddy bear sitting in it.

"Lainie…is that the one I gave you? Your Valentine bear?"

Her heart was beginning to race. She'd dreamed of this moment for so many years, and now that it was here, she was scared of how he would react.

"Yes, it is. Would you bring it to me, please, and then sit down with me for a bit?"

"Sure thing," he said as he picked it up and then sat down and put it in her lap. "Here you go, darlin'. Kinda cool to know you still have it."

Lainie's hands were trembling as she picked it up and laid it in his arms. "The ashes of our son are in a tiny brass heart inside this bear. You're holding your son, Hunt. It's not much of him…but it's all I have left to give you."

Hunt's heart stopped with a kick, and then raced to catch up. He could no longer hear the storm, or the rain pounding on the roof. He couldn't see her face for the tears.

The brown pelt was soft beneath his fingers. The bear's shiny black eyes seemed to be looking at him, and right where a heartbeat would be, he felt the tiny metal heart.

"Jesus, Lainie. Oh, my God. Oh, my God." Then cradled it to his chest and broke into sobs.

She wrapped her arms around him, holding him and the little bear until he had no tears left to cry, and the silence was deafening. Without a word, he reached for her, pulling her into his lap, and rocked her and the bear where he sat.

She hurt for the shock that had untethered him, and for grief she knew all too well. Finally, she moved enough to see his face.

"Look at me, love. This isn't your fault. It wasn't our war. And when you disappeared, I wasn't sure I'd ever see you again. But I hoped. You gave me the bear, and then you gave me the baby, and even after I lost you both, I had the solace of knowing that what was left of him was within the last thing you gave me...like he was being held in your arms for safekeeping."

Hunt knew if he opened his mouth that he'd choke on the words, so he just shook his head and hid his face against the curve of her neck.

"This is so painful for you because it's new. But the day your mother came to my hospital room to tell me she didn't know where you were, and how sorry she was, her words became noise in my head. After she left I cried until I made myself sick. We've been through hell, Hunt. We were so lost...and now we're not...because of you. You found me. You saved me. It's okay to grieve. It's the only thing that will heal, and in the meantime, I'm your backup. A little the worse for wear, but I'm here, and I'm not ever losing you again."

Hunt took her words into his soul. She'd always been his compass to sanity, but he'd seen the warrior she'd become. He already knew how fiercely she fought for who she loved. In his world, it was the people who had your back that mattered most, and she was it. He took a breath, cleared the tears from his face in two angry swipes, and then looked her in the eyes.

"Thank you, darlin'...for holding on to who we were. So, this is who we are, and now it's up to us to create who we're going to be."

"Happy. We're going to be happy," she said.

As they sat, sheltered from the ongoing storm and the rain blowing against the windows, Hunt had a flash of déjà vu.

It was the rain!

Just like the day he lost her.

He'd been standing in the rain, waiting for a phone call that never came. And now they'd come full circle. She was in his arms again.

When she fell asleep in his lap, he carried her to her bedroom with the little bear and covered them with the blanket draped across the foot of the bed. As he was turning to walk away, he noticed something framed, hanging above the bed. He took a step closer, and then stared in disbelief.

His last text to her! She'd seen it, after all. And kept it.

He looked down at her then, healing wounds and bruises, curled up on her side in such a state of peace, with the Valentine bear tucked beneath her chin. She kept saying that he'd saved her, but it was her who saved him.

He left the room, taking care to leave the door open in case she called, then went into the kitchen to call his boss.

Pete Randolph answered on the second ring.

"Hello."

"Pete, it's me, Hunt."

"Hey! I've been expecting you to call. We've been keeping up with your search through the news. We know the hiker was arrested. His first alibi fell through like a rock, didn't it?"

"Yes, sir," Hunt said.

"Congratulations on finding your girl. I hope she's okay."

"Thanks, and yes, she is. She has some healing to do, but she's getting there. The reason I'm calling is to let you know I'm not coming back. I'm staying in Denver with Lainie."

"I'm sorry to hear this, but I'm not surprised. I could tell she meant a lot to you, and we all wish you the best. Your last check will go into your bank account as always. Take care, son, and have yourself a happy life."

"Thank you for everything," Hunt said, and then stood in the middle of the room, trying to decide what to do next.

Food would be happening, but he didn't know what was here, and she'd been missing so long, some things might have expired, or gone bad. So he began going through the pantry to see what was available, then he dug through the contents of her refrigerator before sitting down to make a list.

It became obvious they would order in for supper, but he'd wait to talk to her about the groceries. He didn't know if she did her own shopping, or ordered online for them to be delivered. There were so many little day-to-day things they were going to learn about each other. It was an exciting thought. All the days ahead of sharing laughs and frustrations—of having someone to come home to. It was Hunt's dream of heaven on earth, and it was coming true.

Fort Liberty North Carolina

A TABLE FULL of soldiers were on base, eating their evening meal and trading digs and laughs with their buddies in between mouthfuls of food. Wall-mounted televisions provided the background for their meals and conversations, while what was airing wasn't always noticed.

An evening news show was airing a follow-up to their

previous story about the missing hiker in Colorado, celebrating the fact that she had been found and rescued by none other than a man from her hometown of New Orleans. They went on to explain that the man, an ex-Army helicopter pilot named Hunter Gray had been her childhood sweetheart. The news anchors were listing a quick rundown of his attributes, then followed up by making a joke about "Hollywood will come calling on this story!" when one of the men sitting at that table— a chopper pilot they called Rat—jumped up from his seat, pointing.

"Did you hear that? Did you hear that?" Rat shouted.

T-Bone frowned. "Hear what?"

Rat was running around the table with his fork still in his hand, shouting every word that came out of his mouth. By now, he had the attention of every person in the room.

"The guy who found that missing hiker lady in Colorado! It was Gator! Gator, by God, Gray found her! Using the skills he'd learned in the Army, they said. A former warrant officer with the freaking 82nd Airborne Division, they said! His childhood sweetheart, they said! Hot damn, y'all. That's why he mustered out. He'd left his woman behind, and he, by God, went and found her!"

The room erupted in cheers!

Rat and T-Bone were hugging and slapping each other on the back. Cherokee and Memphis were grinning from ear to ear. Dallas and Roadrunner were high-fiving Cowboy. Tulsa and Chili Dog were staring at the TV in disbelief. Everyone in the room who'd served with him was cheering. Everyone who'd even heard of the ace gunner from the 82nd Airborne was on their feet cheering and whooping. Gator Gray had represented!

NEARLY TWO WEEKS had passed since Lainie's release from the hospital. She was finally back on her feet for short periods of time, and moving slowly. She'd gotten as far as the living room before needing to sit down, and was still there when she saw a delivery van from a local florist shop pull up in her drive.

A man got out, took a huge floral bouquet from the back of the van and headed toward her house. She could walk, but not walk and carry something like that on her own, so she shouted at Hunt.

"Hey honey! Can you come help? There's a delivery guy coming toward the house."

At that moment, the doorbell rang.

Hunt had been unpacking his things from Flagstaff when she called.

"On the way!" he shouted, and came running through the foyer and straight to the door.

"Delivery for Lainie Mayes."

"Thanks," Hunt said, pulled a five-dollar bill from his pocket and tipped the man as he took the vase then toed the door shut behind him. "Wow, darlin'. These are beautiful! Where do you want them?"

"They're gorgeous, and that's the biggest bouquet I've ever seen! How about the dining table? We'll see it every time we walk past, and it's big enough to accommodate it."

"Good call," he said, and headed for the dining room

with Lainie right behind him. He put down the vase then pulled the card and handed it to her, then saw her eyes widen in surprise.

"Oh, honey…oh my… I think these are for you as much as for me. Look," she said, and handed him the card.

For Gator's girl,
Rat, T-Bone, Roadrunner, Memphis, Cowboy,
Tulsa, Chili Dog, Cherokee and Dallas, and the
82nd Airborne, sending our love.
Gator Gray…you did good.

Hunt was stunned. "Never thought I'd hear from them again."

Lainie was elated. This was part of who he'd been, and evidence of how much they'd thought of him.

"We've been all over national news for some time. That's probably how they found out. And that last update I saw, news anchors were really playing up your Army background and the childhood sweetheart connection." She hugged him. "They love you, Hunt. Maybe not as much as I do, but they love you, and you made them proud."

"All I wanted was to find you alive. The flowers are for a special lady, and that's you." He read the card again, picturing their faces as he saw the names, but then he kept going back to "Gator's girl," and finally frowned.

"Lainie, I don't want you to just be Gator's girl. That should read, 'Gator's wife,' but she doesn't exist, and that's all wrong. Can we talk about getting married?"

Lainie slid her arms around his neck. "You already proposed to me once, remember?"

He frowned. "Yes, and you said we'd walk that road after we got to Tulane."

"Because I still wasn't eighteen, and you know my parents would never have given their consent. I thought we had time." Her voice broke. "I was wrong."

"So, you're a grown-ass woman and I'm asking you again. Will you marry me, darlin'?"

"In a heartbeat."

He grinned. "I love how you play hard to get."

She shrugged. "There's no waiting period in Colorado. You can get a marriage license and get married in the same day, if you want to."

He blinked. "Another plus for this state beside the fact that you're living in it. What kind of ID do we need?"

"A simple driver's license will suffice," she said.

"Do you want the ceremony with all the trimmings?" he asked.

"I just want to be your wife. I want the right to call you husband. But I do want to wait until the bruises are gone before we do it, because when we get someone to take our picture, I don't want to look like I'd been in a dogfight, and have people a hundred years from now wondering why."

Hunt kissed the little scar on her forehead, then ran his thumb along the curve of her chin. "It's a deal. But right now, would you like to take a ride?"

"I'm good with taking a ride. I haven't been out of this house since you brought me home from the hospital, except to have the staples taken out of my head."

"Then let's do it. And wear your fuzzy leopard slippers. They're my favorite," he said.

She laughed. "I'm going to need a few minutes."

"Take all the time you need. We've got the rest of our lives to fix the mess our parents made." But then he thought about her walking back through the house just to get shoes and a jacket, and swung her up into his arms and carried her down the hall and into the bedroom. "Consider it taking a shortcut," he said, brushing a kiss on her lips and leaving the room.

Chapter Eight

When they pulled into the drive-through at Freddy's Frozen Custard and Burgers, Lainie beamed.

"Oh, Hunt! Freddy's! Back home, it was our place to go."

"I know. I saw it the other day when I was picking up groceries. Thought of all the times we spent eating their burgers and fries, and the hot fudge sundaes made with the frozen custard."

"Do you remember what I liked?" she asked.

He frowned. "Darlin'. I remember everything about you."

"Then you order for me," she said.

He pulled up to the speaker. "Two original combos, no onions, extra ketchup for the fries and two large, sweet teas," he said, and then drove around to the pickup window for their order.

He drove them to a nearby parking lot, distributed the food, and then they sat watching traffic as they ate.

"This is so good," Lainie said. "All these years I've lived here, and I've never come to Freddy's."

"We're here now, and we'll be back," Hunt said, and dunked his fry into a puddle of ketchup.

Before long, they began playing the traffic game they used to play when they were teens.

"See that old red truck with the dented fender rattling by? He's headed to Dallas, Texas, to see his grannie on her birthday," Lainie said.

Hunt remembered the game and jumped in. "Yeah? Well, take a look at that black Porsche darting through traffic. It belongs to the banker's wife, but she's on her way to meet a guy on the side, and she's gonna get caught, because the banker found out."

Lainie frowned. "Poor wifey. She should have settled for the Porsche and forgot about extramarital sex."

Hunt snorted. "Darlin'…if somebody's not getting enough of it, they'll always go huntin' for it."

Lainie grinned. "I suppose you have a point, unless you're one of those ladies who's had the best and isn't willing to settle for second-rate. Like me."

He licked a drip of ketchup off his lip and stared. "You didn't—"

"Not even tempted. I kind of turned it off, I think. Did you date?"

"Not even once," he said. "I'm a one-woman kind of guy."

"So…you turned it off, too?" she asked.

"I didn't know how to turn off wanting you. I just made love to you every night in my dreams, and suffered through the reality that you were gone," he muttered.

The faint brush of despair in his voice made her sad all over again for what they'd lost. Timing couldn't be worse. She still looked like she had one foot in the grave, but they were together again, sharing food and space, and a future of possibilities.

She wiped her hands and turned to face him.

"Hunter?"

His eyes narrowed. She never called him by his full name unless it was serious. "Yes, darlin'?"

"I know I promised you a sexy nightgown and a pretty body, but if we turn off the lights and you'll settle for as is, you know how to turn me back on."

He took the statement like a fist to the gut, then inhaled to make sure he was still breathing. "Are you finished with that burger?"

Her whole body quickened. "I can be."

He nodded. "I'll gather up the trash."

Today was a day for moving forward, and this moment had been a long time coming.

The drive home happened faster than when they'd left. No sightseeing, or calling attention to points of interest. Just a heart-racing need to be together.

When they pulled into the garage, Hunt ran to her side of the car and picked her up to carry her inside.

"Honey, I can walk," Lainie said.

"If you can say that again in a couple of hours, then you're on your own. But this is me, clearin' the way to paradise."

She said no more and settled for the bird's-eye view she had of his face. Upside down or backward. Front view or silhouette…he was beautiful in her eyes.

He carried her into the house, all the way down the hall to their bedroom before he put her down.

"I'm going to wash up first, or I'm going to taste like ketchup," she said.

"Fine, but don't wash it all off. I like ketchup, too."

Lainie laughed as she walked into the en suite and shut the door. She knew what he was doing…wanting her to forget about how she looked and remember the fireworks when they were together.

When she came out, the shades were down and the covers pulled back on the bed. He was waiting in the shadows, and when she walked into his arms, the removal of their clothing became a dance.

A head bowed to remove a shirt.

A foot lifted to step out of their pants.

The stroke of his hand down the middle of her back.

The rhythm of his heartbeat against her palm.

The fall of her hair across his arm.

The sensual stroke of his tongue in the valley between her breasts.

The catch in her breath when he stretched out beside her.

The glitter in his eyes as he gazed down upon her.

The scars they bore were both outward and inward, but the bond between them was timeless, unbreakable.

He was the same, and yet different.

It wasn't their first kiss…but it was the last remnant of regret for what had been.

"My darlin' Lainie, you never quit me…even after I quit myself. Words do not exist to explain the depths of what you mean to me."

He had that piercing-eye raptor look again, and she was his willing prey. "I love you, Hunt, and that is all."

His heart was pounding as he moved over her, and then he was inside her. Hard as a rock, and throbbing from the blood rush, he began to move.

She closed her eyes, wrapped her legs around his waist and pulled him deeper. *I am whole again.*

It began like it always had between them—with a slow, steady stroke in perfect rhythm. Their bodies fit, like two halves of a perfect whole, turning up the volume as the need grew stronger.

Minute by minute, they chased the heat, always just a little ahead of them, until feel-good turned into need. Need turned into frenzy, and right in the middle of heartbeat, the slam of a climax, wiping out all sense of thought. In the aftermath, they became each other's anchor until the final quake had stilled.

Still inside her, Hunt rolled onto his back, taking her with him, and within seconds felt the first drops of her tears on his chest.

His voice was but a rumble in Lainie's ear.

"You're crying. Please tell me I didn't hurt you."

"No pain. Tears of joy. Making love to you didn't hurt. It healed."

"Okay then," he said, and slid his hands down the ridge of her spine and cupped her backside.

Lainie felt boneless. She couldn't have moved then if she'd tried, and there they laid, heart to heart, as the minutes passed. She was almost at the point of sleep when she heard him groan, and then move within her.

He was hard again, and still inside her.

She raised up just enough to see his ice-blue eyes catch fire.

"What are you waiting for, Gator?"

"Permission to proceed, ma'am."

"Permission granted."

Three days later

LAINIE DIDN'T HAVE a way to thank each and every person responsible for the flowers from Hunt's squadron, so she turned loose of her ego and had Hunt take a picture of her standing by the bouquet and holding a sign that read,

TO THE GUYS IN GATOR GRAY'S SQUAD-
RON, AND THE 82ND AIRBORNE BATTAL-
ION IN FORT LIBERTY
THANK YOU FOR THE FLOWERS.
WITH LOVE—GATOR GRAY'S GIRL.

And then she posted it on her Instagram account.

There was no denying what she'd suffered. But the sweet smile on her battered face said it all. She'd survived.

The post went viral, but all she cared about was making sure Hunt's friends received her thanks.

That evening, she was in the kitchen chopping up vegetables for a casserole when she heard Hunt's Jeep in the driveway. He'd had two separate interviews today with med-flight services, and she was curious to find out what he thought, and what they'd said.

She heard the front door open, wiped her hands and went to meet him.

"I missed you," she said as she gave him a hug.

"I missed you more," he said, and kissed her soundly.

"Get comfy then come talk to me," she said. "I'm chopping veggies for a casserole."

A few minutes later, he was back in his sock feet, minus the boots and flight jacket, but still wearing the jeans and shirt he'd left home in. He walked up behind her, slid his arms around her waist and kissed the back of her ear.

"I have dreamed of this life with you forever. Still have a need to pinch myself that it's real," he said.

She leaned against him, reveling in the embrace. "Fairy tales were always my favorites when I was little because everyone lived happy-ever-after. And I'm also hardheaded. I refused to give up on this dream. I didn't know how it would happen, but I wanted you back in my life."

"And you got me," Hunt said, then reached over her shoulder and grabbed a carrot chunk and popped it in his mouth.

"Give me a couple of minutes to finish this so I can get it in the oven," she said.

"Need help?"

"I might like to look at you now and then while I work, so feel free to lurk about. Grab yourself something to drink, love. I've been standing long enough. I need to sit down soon."

He nodded, took a longneck beer from the fridge, popped off the cap, took a quick sip, and then carried it to the window overlooking her backyard.

"Looks like rain coming in. Earlier, I thought I could smell it in the air," he said.

"I like the rain when I'm snuggled in at home. Not

crazy about driving to work and back in it," she said, and dumped the veggies she'd just cut into the brown sauce on the stove, stirred it all together, then poured it over the seared beef tips in the casserole dish, covered it with foil and put it in the oven. She set the timer for an hour, then started to clean up when Hunt turned around and noticed what she was doing.

"I can do that, darlin'," he said, and set her down with his beer.

She didn't argue. And she had a confession to make.

"I posted the thank-you card photo on Instagram this morning. I don't know if any of the guys have seen it yet, but one hundred forty-three thousand other people have."

He turned, staring at her in disbelief. "What? Are you serious?"

She nodded.

He grinned. "Proper southern lady that you are, that is one hell of a thank-you card."

"The spirit of my grandmother Sarah would have haunted me for life had I not sent a thank-you of some kind. One of her well-repeated adages was 'Proper ladies must have proper manners.'"

He gave her a look. "Well, I don't need a damn thing about you to change. In my eyes, you've always been perfect, and the improper parts are what I love most."

He winked, then finished loading the dishwasher and wiped down the counters.

"Let's go sit where it's comfortable," Lainie said. "I want to put my feet up."

"Uber coming up," Hunt said. "Bring my beer." He scooped her up in his arms.

"You don't have to keep doing this," she said.

"What if I like it?" he said, and then carried her out of the room, eased her down on the sofa so she could stretch out her legs, then sat at the other end and put her feet in his lap. "There now, darlin'. Is that better?"

"Very much so," she said, and handed him his beer. "Now, tell me about your day."

He began lightly rubbing the tops of her feet as he talked. "Both interviews were good. Both companies offer about the same package. I also checked into EMS pilots for hospitals. It's three straight days of twelve-hour shifts, and then six days off. I have the hours, skill and experience to qualify."

"You choose. This is home base. This is where you go when you're not in the air. As long as I'm still Gator's girl, all will be right in my world."

"Gator's wife," he corrected.

She smiled. "Yes…that."

He nodded. "I'm leaning toward the EMS thing. I'll see what's available, and go from there."

"I have something to talk to you about, too," Lainie said. "It's about the baby's ashes."

His hands were still on her feet when he looked up. "What about them?"

"In the beginning, I kept them because of you. I always thought you'd come looking for me one day, and I wanted to give you that moment."

His fingers swept across the tops of her feet and curled around them.

"You did, and I am so grateful."

"But now, every time you see the little bear sitting in the rocker, does it make you feel sad? Is it a hard reminder of the loss, or does it give you comfort to keep it?"

He glanced at the rocker, and then back at her. "What are you asking, darlin'?"

She took a breath. "If you want to lay him to rest."

"What do you want?"

"I don't want to ever hurt you, but in my heart, I feel like keeping the ashes in view, even though we're the only ones who know they're there, isn't fair. Every day we work on putting the past behind us, but it will always be with us, because it was part of our journey. I don't have to hold ashes to remember I carried your child. And our baby was already in the arms of angels before they pulled me out of the wreck."

"You want to scatter them?" he asked.

Lainie's eyes welled. "No. I want to leave the ashes right where they are, and bury the teddy bear. I would like remembering him that way."

Hunt took a deep breath, swallowing past the lump in his throat. "There are days when I think you couldn't get any dearer to me, and then you up and say something like this. You break my heart...in a thousand little pieces. And I would have given anything if you'd never been hurt like this. But you are right. He'll always be with us. We should do this."

Lainie swung her legs off the sofa and then scooted up beside him. "But no funeral service. Just us and a preacher at the gravesite, okay?"

He hesitated. "With one request."

"Name it," she said.

"That I'm his pallbearer."

She nodded. "It is your right."

THAT NIGHT, Lainie was already in bed when Hunt came out of the bathroom. She could smell the scents of his shampoo and body wash as he crossed the room and slid into bed beside her. Her silence was telling, and he knew what it was about.

"I love you, lady, and there is no right or wrong decision here. It's a choice, and if you haven't changed your mind, then we'll start the process tomorrow, okay?"

Her voice was shaking. "And some day, maybe we'll make another baby?"

He kissed the back of her neck. "Well, we certainly know what makes babies, and we do love the practice of it, and I'm damn good at it, so I can't imagine why we'd choose not to."

She chuckled under her breath. "We're going to have to do something about that inferiority complex."

"Hush yourself, girl. You taught me everything I know."

She laughed, then rolled over into his arms. "Well, maybe not everything," she said, and proceeded to prove it.

THE RAIN HUNT predicted came after midnight, and by morning, Denver was sopping wet. Water was still running in the streets when they headed out to Fairmont Funeral Home.

A couple of hours later, after explaining what they

wanted, they purchased plots, chose a casket, ordered a headstone, and set a date and time for the service.

Michael Taylor, the funeral director, had recognized them the moment they walked in, and was quite taken by their request.

"I just want the both of you to know I will do my best to make this service special for you. My deepest sympathies for the tragedy of this loss. I long ago learned there is no expiration date for grief."

"Thank you," Hunt said, and shook his hand. "Until this coming Friday, then?"

"Yes, sir," Taylor said.

THE NEXT FEW days for Lainie were like waiting for the other shoe to drop. She wouldn't even look in the direction of the rocking chair, then one afternoon while Hunt was helping her fold clothes, she caught herself whispering about the service, and was so horrified at herself that she threw her hands up in despair.

"What's wrong with me? Why did I just do that? Like I'm afraid the bear will hear me? Maybe that fall on my head knocked the good sense right out of me!"

He dropped the towel he was folding. "Come here to me, Lainie."

She walked into his arms and laid her head on his chest.

"You're fine," Hunt said. "You know what's happening, right?"

"No, I don't," she mumbled.

He buried his face in the fire of her hair and held her close. "Close your eyes, love, and imagine this scene.

Family and friends have just gathered for a meal after burying Grandpa. At first everyone is quiet and reverent. They get their food and start eating, and they begin to feel better. Somebody mentions how good the food is. And then someone else reminds them of how their people made it different, and then someone else reminds them of how much Grandpa loved pie, and they laugh. And then the shock of having laughed at such a moment when they're supposed to be sad is suddenly an embarrassment, and the room is silent again."

She could see the image he was painting.

"Well, darlin', that's where you are right now. Your reality hasn't caught up with your truth. There's no one left to judge you, and it sure as hell won't be me. And we know ashes don't hold a soul captive. You know that little guy went home a long time ago. And a stuffed bear isn't going to judge you. If toys went to heaven, I think that bear would be happy with the job you have given him."

Her face crumpled. "How did you get so smart?"

"I don't know, darlin'. Maybe it's because I know you better than you know yourself?"

She looked up, and when she did, he kissed her, soft and slow, then set her free.

"You're right," Lainie said. "I'm not second-guessing my choice. I'm just not good at letting go."

"Good. Then that means you won't be one of those wives who has a constant urge to get rid of her husband's treasures…like the old jersey from his football days, and the cleats he wore in the homecoming game."

She blinked. "Do you still have that stuff?"

"I might."

She sighed. "God, how I love you."

"Feelin's mutual, darlin'. Now can I ask you a question?"

"Absolutely," she said.

"Can I have that last piece of lemon pie in the fridge?"

She grinned. "Been eatin' at you, has it?"

"Is that a yes?"

She laughed out loud, and then blinked. "Oh, wow. This is me laughing at the family dinner, isn't it?"

He nodded. "I'll give you the first bite."

"I never could tell you no."

IT WAS THE morning of the funeral. The day was clear, but a little cool. Lainie dressed for warmth, choosing a pair of black winter slacks, a blue cashmere sweater to wear under the matching jacket and soft black socks with a pair of black loafers.

A quick glance in the full-length mirror was the assurance she needed. She mostly looked like herself again. Same long auburn hair hanging below her shoulders. Same arched eyebrows and thick lashes. Same oval face and straight nose. Same lips. Hunt called them kissable. But he also considered her entire body kissable, so there was that. Considering Hunt liked her best naked, then she only had to please herself, and turned away.

Hunt was still in the bathroom shaving, so she went to the kitchen for a cup of coffee. It was hard to figure out how to feel. This wasn't a new loss. And for her, it wasn't fresh grief. Maybe it was about turning loose. Of giving up. All she knew was that the hole in her heart would be real.

She took her coffee to the kitchen table, then sat with her view to the backyard. Before long, the first snow would fall. It wouldn't last. It was just a forerunner of the long winter to come.

She could hear Hunt opening drawers and doors down the hall, and knew he was getting dressed. She smiled. The sound of his presence was her blessing. She would never ask God for more. Then she heard him coming up the hall and turned to look, then forgot to breathe.

He was a sight to behold—the soldier he'd been, in full-dress warrant officer uniform, holding his hat. A black dress jacket, adorned in gold braid and stars. Blue trousers with a gold stripe down the outside of each leg. A white, semiformal shirt with a turn-down collar. A black bow tie. The array of service medals was a road map of his accomplishments, then she saw the Purple Heart. She knew he had one. But she'd never seen it.

He was searching her face for approval. "To honor our son," he said.

Lainie put a hand on her heart. "You honor us all. I don't think I ever said this aloud, but…thank you for your service."

He nodded. "Are you ready, darlin'?"

"Almost," she said.

He followed her to the living room, then to the rocking chair by the hearth. She picked up the little bear, gave it a hug, then handed it to Hunt.

His eyes briefly closed as he held it to him, and then they were gone.

The ride to the funeral home was silent.

Lainie held the bear in her lap all the way, and when they arrived, the director was waiting.

"Follow me," he said, and led them into a viewing room, and up to the tiny, satin-lined casket and the small nosegay of white roses lying on top of it.

Lainie laid the bear inside, as if she was putting a baby to bed, then Hunt stepped forward, and to their surprise, removed his Purple Heart and pinned it onto the bear's chest, right above the metal heart within it.

"He fought his own war," Hunt said.

They were holding hands as the director closed and locked the casket, and then they followed its passage through the winding halls of the funeral home and out to the waiting hearse in the adjoining garage. They stood in silence, watching as the casket and flowers were loaded, and then were escorted to the family car.

Mr. Taylor seated Hunt and Lainie in the back, and as soon as the doors shut behind them, Hunt put his hat in his lap and turned and kissed her.

"This is the hardest day, and you're the bravest person I know. Stay with me, darlin'. I've got your back."

Her eyes were welling with unshed tears, but she had no regrets. "This is why I waited. I could never have done this without you."

"The same people who broke us, broke him. We're free from them now, and he deserves the same level of release."

Mr. Taylor got behind the wheel as the pastor took the seat beside him. The drive was brief, and as soon as they stopped behind the hearse, they all exited the car.

Once again, Hunt was steadying Lainie's steps as they approached the hearse. Upon their arrival, he handed Lainie over to the director.

"Mr. Taylor, I would appreciate it if you would steady my lady's steps. She's still healing from her ordeal."

"It would be my honor," Taylor said, and offered Lainie his arm.

Hunt put on his hat, then leaned into the back of the hearse and picked up the casket. There was a brief moment of clarity as he measured the weight of it. The pack he'd carried throughout basic training weighed thrice this, maybe more, but the absence of life within it was a weight he would forever bear.

He'd already seen the little tent on the hill where the grave had been dug and started toward it, with the rest of the entourage behind him.

He would remember later, the crunch of dead grass and pebbles beneath his feet. Sunlight glittering on a tombstone in the distance, the chill of the wind against his face, and then they were there. With yet another step of the finality of the moment, he set the little casket on the framework of the casket lowering system and moved back to her.

The pastor they didn't know began reading a psalm.

Lainie was weeping silently.

Blinded by his own tears, Hunt reached for her hand.

The act of burial was the final rite of passage, and Hunt was moving through the service in the same way he'd followed orders—in duty and silence.

Eleven years he'd been a father without knowing it.

The unborn child had been given his name, and today, he carried him to the grave.

Hunter James Gray II had never taken a breath, or let out a cry, but today, his mother and father were crying for him.

And then the pastor stopped talking.

The grave attendants moved to the CLS and began lowering the casket until it stopped.

Lainie stepped forward, picked up a handful of dirt from the grave and tossed it onto the casket. Hunt did the same, and then they stood vigil at the site until all of the dirt had been replaced.

In her heart, they'd just put their baby to bed. Leaving it behind was the hard part for her, but he was already with the angels. This parting was for them.

The white roses were on the grave now, and they were driving a temporary grave marker into the ground when Hunt heard Lainie moan beneath her breath, then grab his arm to steady herself. One look, and he knew she was done.

"Darlin', are you hurting?"

She nodded. "I've been standing too long."

Hunt looked around for Taylor, and then called out to him.

"Sir, I need to get Lainie home."

Taylor jumped into action and headed toward the car, as Hunt swung her up in his arms.

"I'm sorry," she whispered. "All of a sudden, I just gave out."

"You don't apologize to me. Doing this for you is my joy."

The director took them back to the funeral home and pulled up beside their Jeep.

"Here you are, but can I get you anything before you leave? Some water, maybe?"

"We have some in the Jeep," Hunt said, "but thank you for everything."

"This is a service I will never forget," the director said.

"You gave us everything we asked for. It was perfect," Lainie said.

"We are always here for you," Taylor said, and drove away.

"I can walk from here," Lainie said.

"Yet, I will carry you," Hunt said, and the moment she was in the seat, he slipped the shoes from her feet, and then brushed a kiss across her lips.

"Buckle up, darlin'. We're going home."

Chapter Nine

The ensuing week was about moving forward.

Hunt carried the little rocking chair to the attic, and Lainie put a potted plant in its place.

After a last trip to Dr. Wagner, he declared her feet healed and cleared her to return to work. She was put back on the roster for the following Monday, but her car had been sitting in the garage for so long that Hunt took it to a garage to be serviced before she started driving it again.

"You're as handy to have around as a pocket on a shirt," Lainie said, when he came back and dropped the car keys in her hand.

"If I'm gonna be a pocket, I want to be the one on the backside of your pants," he said, and kissed her soundly.

She laughed and the Universe took her joy, bound it with a thousand others and sent it out into the world.

He was still reeling from the joy on her face as he stroked the tip of his finger along her cheek. "No bruises left."

"I know. I'm me again," she said.

"Are you ready to take another ride?" he asked.

It was the tone in his voice. "Where to?" she asked.

"The courthouse. To get that marriage license."

Lainie gasped. "Yes, oh yes, but my hair's a mess. I need to change clothes, and…"

He pulled a little black velvet box from the pocket of his flight jacket and opened it, revealing the diamond-encrusted wedding band inside.

Her throat tightened with emotion. "Oh, Hunt. It's beautiful. I'll brush my hair and get my purse," she said, then bolted.

He shouted down the hall, "I expect the same level of excitement when I take you to bed tonight!"

He could hear her laughing, and wondered what her reaction would be when she found out he would be flying choppers for the National Park Service in Denver. After their diligence in searching for Lainie, he liked the thought of being part of that.

Two hours later, they were standing in the corner of the court clerk's office, before a justice of the peace. Lainie was holding a bouquet of daisies, still wrapped in the cellophane from the supermarket, while the lines of people in the clerk's office waiting to be served, now stood as witnesses.

They'd already figured out who the bride and groom were. Everyone knew her name. And their story. And now they were seeing them in the flesh, witnessing their marriage.

Phones were recording the vows. Pictures were being taken. And when Hunter Gray slipped the ring on her finger and kissed his wife for the very first time, there wasn't a dry eye in the room.

"We're married! We're finally married," Lainie whispered.

"And I get to call you my wife," Hunt said.

"Gator's wife," she corrected. "We need another picture to send the guys!" She turned to face the crowd. "Wedding pictures! Will somebody take pictures of us?"

The volunteers were endless. Pictures were taken on both of their phones, and Lainie thanked them profusely when they gave them back.

"I'd throw my bouquet, but I'm pretty sure these daisies are on their last legs. All I'd do is make a mess for somebody else to clean up, so I'm going to take them home and let them shed on my table."

"And, without a threshold to carry her over, I'll have to settle for the exit," Hunt said, then swooped her up in his arms and carried her out the door.

VIDEOS AND PHOTOS with accompanying stories were hitting the internet before they even got home, but they wouldn't have cared. Their plans involved making love, and opening that bottle of champagne they'd been saving, and making love, then emptying the bottle.

Their wedding dinner was pizza with everything, compliments of SliceWorks and served by DoorDash. There were no pictures involved. They weren't wearing enough clothing for modesty's sake.

BACK IN NEW ORLEANS, a little gray-haired lady named Millie Swayze was sitting in her recliner with her feet up, a laptop in her lap and a bowl of cheese puffs beside her, eating away as she scrolled through Facebook.

When she came to a post she'd been tagged in, she stopped and read it.

Check it out. Meant to be, her friend said, and attached a video.

Millie clicked it. The images of the people in the video were a little fuzzy, and the sound wasn't great, but when she realized what she was seeing, and who they were, she started laughing and crying.

"Praise the Lord! Good for you, babies...good for you! You beat them, and you beat the odds!" She licked the cheese dust off her fingers, then reached for a tissue to wipe her eyes. "Now I can die happy! But in the meantime, I'll be sipping a little wine cooler to toast your long and happy lives."

LAINIE PICKED OUT the best picture from the wedding and once again posted it on social media with the heading...

GATOR AND LAINIE GRAY
WEDDING FINALLY HAPPENED!
UNTIL DEATH DO US PART.
HOOYAH!

This time it was T-Bone who saw the post first, and quickly shared it to the team with a caption. This is how you do happy-ever-after.

WHEN LOCAL MEDIA in New Orleans picked up the final chapter to their story, both sets of parents saw it.

Greg and Tina were in the throes of a divorce, so the news only added to the bitterness between them. The acrimony within their lives had destroyed their marriage, destroyed their family, and coming from old money wasn't enough to save their name. And the worst blow of all was that in spite of everything they'd destroyed, they'd never been able to change their daughter's heart.

Lainie loved with a passion far stronger than their hate.

CHUCK AND BRENDA hadn't changed their spots. He was driving a forklift at a warehouse down by the river, and Brenda was waiting tables four days a week. They came home angry and went to bed drunk, still following the path of least resistance. Knowing Hunt and Lainie were married was what they'd expected to happen. There was no coming back from their part in any of it. They'd lost his love when they broke his trust, but if their son was happy, then it was enough.

IT WAS STILL dark when Hunt kissed Lainie goodbye.

"Happy first day back at work," he whispered, and pulled the covers up over her shoulders.

"What time is it?" she mumbled.

"You still have a couple of hours before your alarm goes off. Love you, darlin'. I'll be late coming home."

"Doesn't matter, as long as you do. Love you forever. Fly safe."

"Always," he said, and then he was gone.

She listened until she heard his Jeep starting up, and then rolled over and closed her eyes.

WHEN SHE WOKE up again, the house was quiet. She rolled over and stretched, then threw back the covers and headed for the shower. The rat race was on.

When she got into the car and backed out of the garage, it felt strange to be back behind the wheel, but that sensation quickly faded. By the time she got to the hospital and parked, she could have almost convinced herself it had all been a horrible nightmare, but for Hunt's presence in her life and the ring on her finger.

From the time she entered the building, all the way to the staff lockers, she was greeted with big smiles and warm hugs. When she got to her office, there were flowers on her desk.

She pulled the card and smiled: *Love you, Hunt*

After that, the morning flew by. When it came time for lunch, she headed to the cafeteria.

Charis saw her coming and waved, indicating she'd saved her a chair.

The moment Lainie sat down with her tray, Charis squealed. "Girl…you're all over social media, and you beat me to the altar. Let me see that ring!"

Lainie lifted her hand, eyeing the circlet of diamonds glittering on her finger.

"It's so you," Charis said. "Gorgeous, elegant and understated. I was kind of hoping Hunt would drop by with you."

"He left for work before I did. He sent flowers. They're on my desk."

"Oh, wow! What's he doing?"

"Flying helicopters for the National Park Service here in Denver."

Charis leaned in and lowered her voice. "Can we talk about Randall for a sec?"

Lainie frowned. "Only if it's bad news for him."

"He got ten years with no possibility of parole, and there are other women who've come forward to file similar charges against him."

Lainie picked up her fork and jammed it into the slice of meat loaf on her plate. "Shame they don't still hang people," she said, and popped the bite into her mouth.

Their lunch was quick, and they both headed off in separate directions—Charis back to the fourth floor, and Lainie to set up for an MRI. After that, time passed quickly.

Lainie clocked out and headed for her car. Winter hours made for short days of daylight, and she still needed to go by a supermarket before she went home. Even the simple act of shopping for Hunt was a joy. She had a husband she loved to take care of.

He liked Snickers bars and Pepsi, and big salads with everything in them. He didn't like anything to do with peppermint, and loved her soaking tub, and Creole blackened fish, fried a little on the crisp side.

She drove home in the dark, and was grateful when the garage light came on as she was pulling in. Once the door was down, she carried in the groceries, then paused to flip on the wall switch to the gas fireplace as she headed to her room to change. Within seconds, flames were dancing behind the glass.

It was habit that made her look toward the end of the hearth. Little bear had always been there to greet her, but no more. She sighed, then put her hand over her heart.

"It's okay, baby…you're in here now," she whispered, then went down the hall to change clothes.

She wasn't sure when Hunt would get home, but when he did, she'd be waiting. This was their new normal, and it was good. As soon as she changed, she hurried back to the kitchen and started making a roux. It would take a good thirty minutes to get the dark, rich flavors she was looking for. She'd bought shrimp that had already been cleaned, and had all of the other components on the shelf, or in the freezer. This was the perfect night for some Creole gumbo and rice.

A couple of hours later, gumbo thick with shrimp, okra and andouille sausage was simmering on the back burner, rice was in the steamer and a pitcher of sweet tea was in the fridge. She'd already had a shower and changed into warm sweats and fuzzy socks, and was sitting in the recliner with a glass of tea when she saw headlights flash through the curtains.

Her heart skipped. He was home.

HUNT CAME RUSHING into the house, trying to outrun the cold before it snuck in behind him. Even as he was closing the door, she was coming to meet him.

"Louisiana in the house!" he said, then kissed her soundly. "Thank you, Lord, for the woman I come home to," he said. "What is that heavenly smell?"

Lainie grinned. "You mean besides me? It could be the gumbo simmering on the stove."

All the teasing ended. The smile slid off his face, and then he hugged her.

"What's that for?" she asked.

"In Iraq... I dreamed of gumbo and rice, and endless glasses of sweet tea."

She shivered. "Talk about being on the same wavelength. That's our dinner tonight."

He hugged her again. "Is it done…ready to eat?"

"Yep."

"Lord, have mercy…give me a few," he said, and bolted down the hall.

"I'll just be in the kitchen," she said, to no one listening, and went to get the pot of gumbo off the burner.

She had dishes at the ready, glasses filled and rice in the bowls when he came back.

He leaned over to smell the gumbo and closed his eyes. "It smells as good as you look," he said, then kissed the back of her neck. "You worked all day, and then it's obvious you've been working ever since you came home. You sit. I can ladle gumbo over rice without making a mess."

"Deal," she said, and carried their glasses to the table, then watched the play of muscles on his back as he dipped and poured.

He carried the bowls to the table, then sat down beside her. "I gotta taste this before we start talking," he said.

"It's hot. Don't burn your mouth."

He winked. "Yes, ma'am."

Since he'd been warned, the first taste was tentative, but from the look on his face when he chewed and then swallowed, Lainie knew she'd hit a home run.

"Darlin', I'm not just blowing smoke here. This might be the best gumbo I've ever had. Thank you for making this. You brought us home."

"You are most welcome, love. Enjoy. We can talk later."

He nodded, and took another bite, scooping rice and gumbo, and going through two glasses of tea before his bowl was empty.

"I'm gonna want seconds, but I gotta sit a minute to let it settle."

She grinned. "So, what was your day like? Do you think you're going to like it?"

"Yeah, what's not to like? I'm in the air. No one's giving me orders. No one's shooting at me. I flew some people from the Department of the Interior in DC back and forth over a specific area they wanted to see. Something to do with new growth from an old burn zone. What about you? Did you make it okay? Did your feet bother you?"

"I was fine, and some sweet man sent me flowers. They were on my desk when I arrived. Thank you, honey. You are the best. Oh… Charis thinks my ring is beautiful, and she thinks you are, too."

Hunt sat, watching the way her expressions changed with what she was saying, and how green her eyes looked when she wore blue, and how soft her hair was against his skin when they made love. She was all soft and southern sweet until threatened or crossed. Unleashing the wild in a redheaded woman was a dangerous thing, but she was everything he wanted.

He ate that second bowl of gumbo before they cleaned up the kitchen. They made love on a rug in the firelight before taking themselves to bed. Even as she was curling herself against him, he wanted her again, but it was late, and there was always tomorrow.

THERE WAS SNOW on the ground, and Christmas was in the air.

Hunt and Lainie had just put up their first tree together, and had two different Christmas parties on the calendar to attend. Their world was expanding—their lives growing richer—and fuller, in more ways than one.

LAINIE WAS SITTING on the edge of their bathtub, staring down at the test stick she was holding—waiting. The sensation of déjà vu was so strong she couldn't breathe without wanting to cry.

She kept muttering, "Please, God, please. Let it be. Let it be."

She kept glancing at the time, and was so scared at one point that she thought she was going to faint, and put her head between her knees. Afraid to look. Afraid not to. Then the feeling passed, and when she looked up, she had an answer.

"Oh, my God," she mumbled, and started to cry, then headed for the living room.

HUNT WAS KICKED back in the recliner with his feet to the fire, half-listening to the music Lainie had playing in the kitchen. The weekend was always the best, because that's when they had time off together, even though he'd been grounded for two days because of a blizzard, and it was still snowing. He was watching snow fall outside the windows when he heard Lainie coming up the hall. He glanced up as she walked in, saw the tears on her face, and was on his feet and moving toward her.

"Darlin', what's wrong? Are you hurt. Are you sick?"

She held out the test stick. "No, I'm just pregnant. We're going to have a baby, Hunt. Merry Christmas, love. You're going to be a daddy."

Hunt froze, then an explosion joy rolled through him. Seconds later, she was in his arms.

"Oh, my God, Lainie, this is wonderful! Are you happy? Please be happy."

She was laughing through tears. "Yes, I'm happy. I still dream of a little version of you."

He smiled. "Or a little version of you," he said softly.

She put her hand on his chest, feeling the steady hammer of his heartbeat against her palm. "It doesn't matter. All I know is you gave me another baby to love. You're my lifeline to joy. Merry Christmas, Gator."

"Merry Christmas, darlin'," he murmured, then lowered his head and kissed her.

* * * *

Suspended.

The dreaded word reverberated like a drumbeat inside Detective Sydney Shepherd's head, keeping time with the dull throb from her concussion. Her stomach churned as she mentally replayed the high-speed chase that had culminated in a single vehicle car crash and a trip to the nearest ER.

The ER doctor had been blunt. *You're lucky to be alive, young lady.*

Yeah, no kidding. Not that she needed his censure. She'd done nothing but berate herself since crawling through that broken window.

What were you thinking, pursuing a vehicle at that speed?

I was thinking I wanted to catch a killer before he fled the country. I was thinking I wanted to wipe that smug smile from Gabriel Mathison's face once and for all. I was thinking of that moment when I could finally slap the cuffs on his wrists and read him his rights.

She lay flat on her back and stared at the ceiling in gloomy silence. *You deserve every bit of this misery. Thanks to you, Gabriel Mathison is now untouchable.*

He's probably out there at this very moment celebrating his victory.

"Syd? Did you hear what I said?"

She dropped her gaze from the ceiling to the middle-aged man at the foot of the bed. Drawing a painful breath, she released it slowly. "Yes, I heard you. You said I'm suspended without pay pending a full investigation."

"I said more than that." For a moment, Lieutenant Dan Bertram let his professional demeanor slip, and a fatherly concern flickered across his careworn features. "Are you in a lot of pain?"

She used every ounce of her strength not to groan. "Nothing I can't handle."

His tone turned gruff. "You don't have to do that, you know. Pretend you're unbreakable. This is me you're talking to. I used to patch up your skinned knees when you were little."

"Okay, even my eyeballs hurt. Is that what you wanted to hear?"

"If it's the truth. When I got the call…" He paused as a myriad of emotions flashed across his features. "They sent me a photo of your car. I didn't know what to expect when I walked through that door."

"I'm sorry to worry you. The doctor says I'll be fine."

"Thank God for that." He seemed to wear the weight of the world on his slumping shoulders as he stood gazing down at her. His uniform was starting to tug across the middle, and beneath his receding hairline, his brow had deepened into a perpetual scowl. Before Sydney's dad had died, the two men had been partners and best friends. Dan Bertram had been her godfather long before he'd become her mentor and finally her commander. He expected a lot from her, and his obvious disappointment was a hard pill for Sydney to swallow.

"It could have been worse," she said.

"Much worse," he agreed. "You're young. You'll heal. And the suspension isn't permanent."

"We both know that's a mere formality. Even if by some miracle I'm allowed to stay on the force, I'll be busted down to patrol or desk duty. I'll never be allowed anywhere near the Criminal Investigations Unit again. Richard Mathison will see to that. He promised to rain hell down upon me if I went after his son. It wasn't an idle threat."

"Yet you went after him anyway."

"I followed the evidence. You would have done the same."

The lieutenant sighed. "We're talking about you right now and the consequences of your actions. I'll ask the chief to have a word with Mathison. They're old friends. Maybe she can get him to call off the dogs. Avoiding a lawsuit will go a long way toward rehabilitating your reputation within the department."

Sydney wasn't buying it. "Why would the chief go out on a limb for me? Why would you, for that matter? You've got your own career to consider."

"Don't worry about me. I know how to protect myself. As to the why, I made a promise years ago that I'd look out for you, and I don't go back on my word. Besides..." A rare smile tugged at his mouth. "I see something of my younger self in you. I know what it's like to have a fire in your belly. That burning need to make a name for yourself. I know how dangerous it can be, too. Your dad cut me a break once when I was still green and ambitious, and I'm willing to do the same for you, on one condition."

Her gaze narrowed. "What?"

"Use your recovery time to reflect on your choices. I'm dead serious about that. You need to reevaluate your priorities. Your dad set a high bar, and no one knows better than I the difficulty of living up to Tom Shepherd's standards." He leaned in. "But here's the thing you need to remember. He wasn't born a hero. His legacy wasn't created overnight. He made mistakes along the way just like everyone else. You've been a detective for less than two years. You've still got a lot to learn. If Tom were here now, he'd be the first to tell you that patience and discretion are virtues. You have to know when to back off."

The advice didn't sit well with Sydney. She didn't like being manipulated, nor did she believe for a moment that her dad would have let a guy like Gabriel Mathison walk because his family had clout and money. "You mean back off when the suspect has a wealthy father who also happens to be a member of the city council?"

The lieutenant's demeanor hardened in the face of her defiance. "It's called politics. It's called living to fight another day. You let your emotions get the better of you this time. You became so single-minded in your pursuit of Gabriel Mathison that you allowed him to goad you into making it personal."

Anger bubbled up in her despite her best efforts. She took a calming breath and counted to ten. "Mathison thinks he's above the law. He thinks he can get away with murder because of who his father is. You and I both know he killed Jessica King. He attacked her with a blunt-force instrument, strangled her while she lay unconscious and dumped her body on the side of the road. Then he partied with his friends for the rest of the night. If that isn't cold-blooded, I don't know what is."

"Knowing and proving are two different things. And, unfortunately, those same friends have given him an alibi for the time in question."

"Then we need to break them. We need to persuade one of them to come forward and tell the truth."

"You've tried that already."

"Obviously, I didn't try hard enough. That's on me." She paused to tamp down her emotions yet again. "I know you don't want to hear this, but what if I'm right? What if Jessica King wasn't his first victim? He has a violent history that his father has worked very hard to conceal. What if Gabriel Mathison was the perpetrator of at least two other unsolved homicides in the past eighteen months?"

Her steely resolve deepened his scowl. "You're right. I don't want to hear it. That's the kind of overreach that got you into trouble in the first place."

"I know that."

"Do you? Because your actions suggest otherwise." She tried to protest, but he put up a hand to halt her. "Just listen for once. Your first homicide investigation could have been a big opportunity for you, but you went too far. You couldn't nail Mathison on the case you were assigned, so you started digging for connections that were at best weak and at worst far-fetched. You acted impulsively and some might say irrationally, and now here we are."

His blunt assessment of her performance was like a dagger through her heart. Turning her head to the narrow window, she fixed her gaze on the parking lot while blinking back hot tears. "Do you really think it's a coincidence that Jessica King's best friend was transferred to another state after claiming Jessica was afraid of Gabriel Mathison? Or that the witness who saw a physical altercation between Gabriel and Jessica the night she was murdered suddenly decided to recant her story? Richard Mathison is cleaning up his son's mess just like he's always done. Why would he go to all that trouble if Gabriel is innocent? Three victims in the last eighteen months, all strangled, their bodies found along the interstate just miles from the Mathison beach house. I suppose that's also a coincidence."

"Think about what you just said. Why would he dispose of bodies so close to his family's property?"

She turned back to him. "Why not, if he thinks he's untouchable?"

"Okay." The lieutenant's voice became deceptively calm, but any hint of patience or support had long since vanished. "Let's go through this one last time. The first victim was found in the trunk of an abandoned car, the second a few months later in a shallow grave. Both had been strangled, both had close ties to the drug trade. That's a dangerous lifestyle. Executions are as common as handshakes. Jessica King was an associate at a respected law firm. She came from a good family with no known ties to the cartels or any other criminal enterprise. Despite your efforts to the contrary, you haven't been able to link her murder to the other two homicides."

"Except for how she was murdered. Two strangulations might be a coincidence but three is a pattern," she insisted.

"You're doing it again, Syd. You just can't help yourself, can you?"

Her chin came up. "All I know is that sweeping inconvenient facts under the rug won't make them go away. Something very real and very dark is happening in our backyard. A killer is out there preying on young women. I don't know how or why, but my every instinct is telling me that Gabriel Mathison is somehow involved."

"That kind of talk doesn't leave this room, Detective." The formality of his admonishment underscored his warning. He was no longer a caring godfather or even a concerned mentor, but a commanding officer putting her on notice. "The last thing we want is to scare the community into thinking we have an active serial killer in the area. As for Mathison…" He straightened and returned to the foot of her bed. "He's no longer your concern. Under no circumstances will you make contact with him. If you pass him on the street, look the other way. From this moment forward, that man is dead to you. Am I clear?"

She swallowed a retort and nodded.

"Keep your mouth shut and your head down until this situation is resolved one way or another. In the meantime, I would advise that you give some thought to what you'll say if and when you go before the review board. Don't get defensive and don't be afraid to show remorse. A little humility can go a long way."

Defiance crept in despite her best efforts. "Even when I know I'm right?"

His icy glare spoke volumes. "Learn to play the game or get used to writing parking tickets."

SYDNEY CONTEMPLATED THE lieutenant's warning while she waited for the doctor to return. Depending on the results of the CT scan, she could be released as soon as her broken bone was set. A night in the hospital was the last thing she wanted. The teeming misery of the emergency room made her long for the quiet sanctuary of her tiny garage apartment.

She also needed access to her laptop. As luck would have it, she'd downloaded her case notes to the hard drive, enabling her to continue a virtual investigation while she recuperated at home.

You're doing it again, Syd. The lieutenant's admonishment lingered like a bitter aftertaste. *You just can't help yourself, can you?*

A nurse came in to recheck her vitals and to inform her that she was being moved to a private room. When Sydney expressed dismay, he gave her a sympathetic smile. "Don't worry. You'll be out of here before you know it. For now, though, we'd like to keep an eye on you overnight. As soon as the order comes through, someone will be in to take you upstairs. That may be a while, though, so just sit tight, okay? We don't want to lose you in all the confusion."

Sydney couldn't tell if he was joking or not.

Forcing herself to relax, she lay back against the pillow and closed her eyes. Surprisingly, she managed to drift off. She had the strangest dream about being wheeled into a section of the hospital under construction and left to fend for herself. When she tried to get up from the gurney, she discovered her wrists and ankles were shackled to the metal bed rails. She couldn't move or call for help. All she could do was watch in horror as a masked surgeon, whose eyes looked an awful lot like Gabriel Mathison's, materialized at her side with what looked to be a bone saw.

She awoke on a gasp.

"You okay?" a voice asked from the doorway.

She turned her head toward the sound. A man stood just inside the room reading a file he'd plucked from the plastic holder on the door. He also wore a mask, but his head was bowed to the chart so that she couldn't see his eyes.

Her pulse accelerated as she watched him. He wasn't the doctor who had examined her earlier nor did he appear to be a nurse or attendant. He didn't look as if he belonged in the hospital at all, dressed as he was in faded jeans, sneakers and a plaid shirt that he wore open over a gray T-shirt. It came to her in a flash that he might be someone the Mathisons had sent to finish her off. She wanted to laugh at her imagination, but knowing what she knew about that family, the notion didn't seem that absurd.

She tried to project authority into her voice. "Who are you?"

He didn't glance up. "I just came by to see how you're doing."

"Are you a doctor?" Something about his voice... about the way he kept his head lowered just enough so that she couldn't get a good look at him... "Where's Dr. Parnell?"

"I'm sure he'll be along soon." He dropped the file back into the holder and turned. "How's the pain?"

"Manageable." She gripped the edge of the bed, realizing how completely at this stranger's mercy she was. She couldn't run, much less fight, though she wouldn't go down without trying. "Who are you again?"

He strode into the room as if he had every right in the world to be there. When he got to the foot of the bed, he removed the paper mask and stuffed it into his shirt pocket.

She gaped at him in astonishment. *"Trent Gannon?"*

His gaze raked her from head to toe. "You remember my name. I'd say that's a good sign, considering the head injury."

She swallowed back her shock. "Not necessarily. Some people are hard to forget under any circumstances."

"Thank you."

"It wasn't a compliment." She forced her gaze to remain steady when she really wanted to glance away from the boldness of his gray eyes. "How did you get back here anyway? They have restrictions on who can come and go from this area."

He shrugged. "I've always found that if you act like you belong, most people are reluctant to question you."

"Someone should speak to security about that," she muttered. *Trent Gannon.* She shook her head in disbelief. "You still haven't told me why you're here."

"I was visiting a friend in the hospital. He had the TV on and I heard about the high-speed chase on the local news." He gave a low whistle. "I decided to come look you up."

"So you can gloat?"

He lifted a brow at her curt tone. "Do you really think I'd take pleasure in someone else's misfortune?"

"Yes, I do. Don't you remember what you said to me the last time we met face-to-face?"

"That was a stressful day." He moved back so that he could lean a shoulder against the wall. His presence filled that tiny room, so much so that Sydney found it a little difficult to catch her breath. She resisted the urge to pull the sheet up to her chin even though she was still fully clothed. "I'd just surrendered my shield and firearm and packed up my desk. I said a lot of things to a lot of people on my way out. But that was a long time ago. I don't hold a grudge."

Sydney bristled. "I should hope not, considering everything that happened was your fault. You had to know you were risking your career when you decided to show up drunk to a crime scene."

Something that might have been regret flickered in his eyes. "When someone starts drinking on the job, they usually aren't thinking too clearly, period."

"I guess not." She hesitated, then said in a softer tone, "For the record, no one enjoyed watching your downfall."

His smile turned wry. "I don't know if that's entirely true."

"It is. A lot of people covered for you for as long as they could. Longer than they should have."

His smile disappeared. "But not you."

She met his gaze without flinching. "I had no choice. I was asked point-blank by my commanding officer what

I'd witnessed at that crime scene. I had to tell the truth. You were becoming a danger to yourself and others."

"You did the right thing."

His response took her aback. He wasn't at all the way she remembered him. He'd once been considered the best detective in the Criminal Investigations Unit, someone who commanded respect and admiration from his peers and superiors alike. But at the height of his career, he'd already displayed a tendency to self-destruct.

In the ensuing silence, she tried to study his demeanor without being obvious. She'd once found Trent Gannon attractive, but that was back when he was still a hotshot detective with an unparalleled record for closing cases. His downward spiral had changed her perception of him and in time he'd become a cautionary tale. Now she found herself unsettled by the similarities to her current trajectory.

"As you said, it was a long time ago," she murmured for lack of anything better to offer.

"Nearly three years," he said with a nod. "I was headed down a bad path. It took me a long time to admit that you actually did me a favor. Losing my job made me take a cold, hard look at myself. I knew I needed to make changes. I had to stop drinking. So I woke up one morning and decided to quit cold turkey."

"That couldn't have been easy."

"It wasn't, but for me, booze was always more of a crutch than a craving. A liquid Band-Aid. I didn't miss it after I quit. I sure as hell didn't miss the hangovers."

"I'm glad you're doing well," she said and meant it, though she wasn't sure if she believed him. "It's admirable that you turned your life around, but I still don't understand what any of this has to do with me."

The inscrutable look he gave her sent a shiver of alarm down her spine. "It's simple. You helped me once. I'd like to return the favor."

"How?"

He came around to the side of the bed and pulled up a stool. "May I?" He sat without waiting for her consent.

She scanned his features, noting the fine lines around his eyes and mouth, the hairstyle that had grown a little too shaggy and the clothing that had seen better days. She wondered suddenly what his life had been like since he'd left the department.

"I've been following your case," he said. "For what it's worth coming from me, I think you're right about Gabriel Mathison. Something is off about that guy. There've been rumors about him for years and how he likes to play rough with women. I don't know if he killed his girlfriend, but he's hiding something."

He had her full attention now. "What do you mean? Give me specifics."

"I can't," he said, quelling her excitement. "It's instinct more than anything else. A gut feeling after watching his body language at his father's press conference. I'm still pretty good at reading people."

"Richard Mathison gave a press conference? That was fast. And...not good," she fretted. "For me, at least."

Trent nodded. "They played it off as improvised, but everyone knows he has the local media in his pocket. Not just the media. Plenty of important people in this town owe him favors. Some of them work for the police department. I've seen firsthand how evidence can disappear and witnesses will clam up after a single phone call from his office. But the kind of money that can be used to bribe and coerce can also make people arrogant and careless. Gabriel Mathison doesn't have his father's discipline. Sooner or later, he'll let something slip. He'll talk to the wrong person. His ego won't allow him to remain silent."

She said on a resigned sigh, "I hope you're right, but I won't be the one to bring him in. I've been removed from the investigation and suspended without pay. If I go near Gabriel Mathison, I face termination and possibly a lawsuit." She cast a worried glance toward the hallway door. "I shouldn't even be talking to you about the case."

He lowered his voice. "I understand. They've put you on a short leash. Forget the nuts and bolts of the investigation. Tell me about the accident."

"Why?"

"I'd just like to hear from you what happened."

Sydney still didn't trust his motives, but for the time being, she decided to give him the benefit of a doubt if for no other reason than the conversation distracted her from the searing pain in her ankle.

"I received an anonymous call that a plane was fueled and waiting on a private airstrip to fly Mathison across the border," she said. "Long story short, I staked out his place and then followed him onto the interstate when he left his house. He accelerated. I accelerated. Next thing I knew, a third vehicle came out of nowhere and cut me off. I swerved, hit the shoulder and rolled."

"Do you think you were set up?"

"I've wondered about that. But how could he have been so certain I'd take the bait, let alone that I'd lose control of my vehicle?"

"He knew you wouldn't take the chance on letting him leave the country. The third car was either meant to take you out or make the pursuit appear more dangerous and reckless than it was. Even without the crash, a high-speed chase would have been enough to trigger an investigation into your conduct. You likely would have been removed from the case regardless."

Sydney grimaced. "He outmaneuvered me. The lieutenant was right. I let my emotions get the better of me and now I'm stuck in here while he's out there free to do as he pleases."

"That's why I'm here," Trent said. "If you're willing to take a chance on me, I can help you nail him."

His offer stunned her. She searched for a telltale crack or twitch in his features as she wondered yet again why he'd turned up out of the blue the way he had. It couldn't be as simple as making amends. "As intriguing as I find the offer, you'll understand why I'm a little concerned about your motive."

"I just want to help."

"Even if I wanted or needed your help, I can't go anywhere near Gabriel Mathison. If I so much as glance at him sideways, my suspension becomes permanent."

"True, but I'm a private citizen. I can do whatever I want within the law. Besides…" He leaned forward, his eyes still shadowed with something she couldn't read.

"We both know you were never going to let this go regardless of the consequences."

"You don't know anything about me."

A faint smile flickered across his face. "I know a driven person when I see one. I'm offering you a way around your suspension. I do all the legwork and conduct the interviews. Your hands stay clean."

She frowned. "What do you want in return?"

He got up and moved back to the foot of the bed, as if what he had to say required a little distance. "For the past couple of weeks, I've been doing a deep dive into a series of murders that occurred in Southeast Texas from the late '90s through the early 2000s. The bodies of seven young women were found in as many years along the I-45 corridor from Houston to Galveston. Are you familiar with those cases?"

"No, but I would have been a little kid back then."

He nodded. "I didn't remember them, either, until I recently interviewed a retired Houston police detective on my podcast. He said—"

She cut him off. "Hold on. Your *podcast*?"

He looked amused. "Not what you expected from a former drunk?"

Hardly. Never in a million years would she have associated Trent Gannon with anything remotely connected to a podcast or social media in general. If someone had told her that he'd been found dead in a ditch somewhere or that he was serving time in a state penitentiary, yeah. Either of those scenarios would have been more believable.

His smile turned deprecating. "I started the podcast

as a side hustle. A way to make a few bucks while drumming up business for my private detective agency—"

She cut him off a second time. "You're a private detective now? Since when?"

"Since I needed to eat and pay bills and no one would hire me," he said with brutal honesty. "I was more surprised than anyone when the podcast took off."

She took a moment to digest his revelations and to adjust her perception of him. Not dead in a ditch or serving time, but a man who'd pulled himself up from a very dark place and carved out a new career for himself. Would she have the courage to do the same?

"The MO on those cases was all over the place. Shootings, stabbings, strangulations—"

Sydney bolted upright despite the bruised rib. Then she clutched her side and eased back down. "Sorry. Please continue."

"Different causes of death and bodies found in different locations. No apparent similarities or connections among the victims. No physical resemblances other than an age range. Nothing in common except for the fact that their murders went unsolved. By every indication, the homicides were random. Each case was investigated individually by the appropriate jurisdiction, and only brief mentions ever appeared on the news or in the papers. Despite the disparities, a detective assigned to one of the cases began to suspect a single killer was responsible, and requested assistance from the FBI. The information gathered from the various law enforcement agencies was consolidated and a common thread eventually identified. Articles of clothing and jewelry had been taken from each of the victims. Initially, it was assumed the items had been lost during captivity or a struggle. An earring, a scarf, a handbag. In every single case, at least one shoe was missing. Always the left shoe."

Sydney rubbed a hand up and down her arm, where goose bumps had suddenly erupted. "Why the left shoe?"

"Possibly some kind of fetish or disorder. Or a misdirection to fool the police." He shrugged. "One victim a year for seven years and then the murders stopped. For whatever reason, the killer went dormant and the trail went cold. Very few people in the area ever realized that a serial predator had lived among them. May still live among us."

Sydney stared at him for the longest moment, almost afraid to say aloud the conclusion she'd immediately jumped to. "Are you suggesting he's active again?"

He seemed hesitant to answer. "It's a long shot. Chances are the killer is dead or in prison for another crime. But my gut tells me that he's still out there. I'm trying to find another piece of the puzzle, no matter how small or seemingly insignificant. You may be able to help me."

"How?"

"Your dad was the local cop who brought in the FBI."

"What?" She pushed herself up against the pillows. "Are you sure?"

"Yes. You didn't know?"

She tried to conceal her shock. The conversation had taken a turn she hadn't expected. "He wouldn't have mentioned anything about it at home. My mother didn't like hearing about his cases."

"That's usually for the best." Something in his tone

made her wonder again about his private life. "The fifth body was found within the Seaside city limits. Your dad took lead. He'd been working the case for over a year when another body turned up in a remote area of Galveston County. Rather than trying to coerce cooperation from the various jurisdictions, he decided to request assistance from the feds."

Sydney sat riveted. "What was the cause of death in his case?"

"Victim Number Five was the first of three strangulations."

"*Three* strangulations?" She tried to fight off a growing uneasiness as something clicked into place. Maybe she did have a vague recollection of those cases. An overheard conversation between her parents niggled at the back of her mind.

Don't let her play outside alone until we catch the bastard.

She's a handful, Tom. I can't watch her twenty-four hours a day.

Trent pounced on her silence. "What's wrong? Did you remember something?"

"Not really. Nothing helpful." But the memory kept tugging. *She's a handful, Tom. I can't watch her twenty-four hours a day.* Even with the threat of a serial killer on the loose?

"Are you sure?" he pressed.

She sighed. "Like I said, I was just a little kid back then. As for my dad, he died a few years ago. And there's no way I can get my hands on his case files, if that's where you're going with this."

"You still have friends in the department, don't you?"

"No one who'll stick their neck out for me."

Except for Dan Bertram, although she'd done a pretty good job of burning that bridge earlier. Trent said something, drawing her attention back to their conversation. "I'm sorry. What?"

"I asked about your dad's notebooks. Did he keep any records at home?"

"His personal belongings were put in storage when I sold the house," she told him. "It would take hours to go through all the boxes."

"I'm willing if you are."

She gave him a long look of scrutiny. "Why didn't you tell me the truth from the start instead of trying to play me?"

"What do you mean?"

Her gaze narrowed. "Admit it. You don't give a damn about helping me. You just want access to my dad's files."

"Why can't it be both?"

At least he didn't insult her with a flat-out denial. "Why are you so interested in these cases anyway? What's in it for you? Are you trying to prove something? Or is it just about content for your podcast?"

"You didn't mention justice."

She folded her arms.

"Okay, you're right. It was about content in the beginning," he admitted. "But the deeper I dug…" He hesitated, as if unsure how much he wanted to reveal. "Let's just say, I now have a more compelling reason for exploring these murders."

"What reason?"

"That's something I'm not yet ready to discuss."

"Being cryptic won't help your case," she warned. "And anyway, I don't know that I'm comfortable letting you dig through my dad's things. He was a very private person."

"Will you at least think about it?"

She gave a vague nod.

He came back around to the side of her bed and stared down at her. "Don't make the mistake of thinking the department will have your back. The moment Richard Mathison files a lawsuit, they'll circle the wagons. You have no idea how bad it can get."

"I'm starting to have an inkling," she murmured.

He removed a card from his shirt pocket and placed it on top of the sheet. "If you find yourself out in the cold, give me a call."

Don't miss
The Killer Next Door
by Amanda Stevens,
available September 2024 wherever
Harlequin® Intrigue books and ebooks are sold.

www.Harlequin.com